OCT - - 2007

THE HEAT OF THE MOMENT

From the moment Angela set eyes on Ryan, she knew he was trouble — the man was a walking invitation to passion! But Angela had no intention of ever falling in love again. So what was it about this arrogant, thoroughly conceited man that made her go weak at the knees? Was she really falling in love? Or was it no more than a passing moment of summer madness?

KAY GREGORY

THE HEAT OF THE MOMENT

Complete and Unabridged

LINFORD
Leicester

First published in Great Britain in 1994

First Linford Edition
published 2007

British Library CIP Data

Gregory, Kay
    The heat of the moment.—Large print ed.—
Linford romance library
    1. Love stories
    2. Large type books
    I. Title
    823.9'14 [F]

ISBN 978–1–84617–793–4

Published by
F. A. Thorpe (Publishing)
Anstey, Leicestershire

Set by Words & Graphics Ltd.
Anstey, Leicestershire
Printed and bound in Great Britain by
T. J. International Ltd., Padstow, Cornwall

This book is printed on acid-free paper

1

'Whew!' Angela peeled off her beige suit jacket and wiped a damp arm across her forehead. 'Do you suppose a cyclone scooped up the office when I wasn't looking, and dumped us smack in the middle of the Sahara? It's not supposed to get this hot in May.'

When nobody answered, she turned towards the desk where her secretary normally sat, and remembered that she didn't have a secretary. 'But I would have one if there wasn't some kind of love virus on the rampage in this building,' she grumbled to the uninterested white walls. 'It's a good thing I'm immune to the infection.'

As Angela's last two secretaries had left the offices of A.P. Baddingley, Attorney-at-Law, to follow the dictates of their hearts, she felt she had reason to be grateful for immunity. Not that

Faith would thank her for referring to Max Kain as an infection, she reflected wryly, remembering the handsome mountaineer with the sexy grin. Neither was Sarah likely to see her love for her husband, Brett, as a bug that needed dosing with antibiotics.

Angela stretched, and crossed the room to stand by the open window. It looked even hotter down there in the street. And love was all very well in its place, but there were times when she wished its place were not her office. Being without a secretary was inconvenient, and so far her advertisements via the Caley Cove grapevine hadn't produced a single eager applicant. Not that she had really expected they would. Young people usually left school and Caley Cove at the same time. Older ones retired to raise a family. Which meant that soon she would have to think about advertising further afield.

The door to Koniski's real-estate office across the road closed with an audible snap, and Angela glanced up, wondering who could have the energy to bang doors in this kind of heat.

A tall, upright figure in jeans and a denim shirt stepped on to the pavement and stood still.

Angela pushed her pink glasses up her nose to peer more closely. Mr Harry Koniski's clientele was looking up. Altogether promising, this one. Wide shoulders, a body that was all muscle and no fat, longish, tawny-gold hair and full, firm lips above a cleft chin and a square, no-nonsense jawline . . . She couldn't quite see the colour of his eyes, but the brows were dark and pronounced . . .

'Angela Baddingley,' she muttered, hastily straightening her spine, 'stop gawking like a moonstruck teenager. You are a thirty-five-year-old, happily divorced lawyer with no desire for any kind of entanglement.'

I know, responded a tiresome voice in her head. But that doesn't mean I'm indifferent to handsome men — especially in Caley Cove, Washington, where even homely men under sixty are in short supply.

The man outside Koniski's shoved his hands deep into his pockets and stood gazing up at the relentless blue of the sky. Was he as hot and uncomfortable as she was? He didn't look it. He looked cool and in control, the sort of man who would hold steady under enemy fire. There was something about him, though, something in the way he was standing, that made him seem unapproachable, private beyond reasonable discretion.

In other words, a challenge. Angela smiled pensively. Except that he was probably married with half a dozen sticky and clamorous kids.

The object of her scrutiny started to cross the road at that moment. He moved with a leisurely, swinging gait that reminded her of a large, tawny cat on its way to pick out a meal. As he came closer, she saw that his eyes were a shadowy grey, and that a small white scar slanted from above his right eye.

A moment later he was directly beneath her window.

That was when Angela Baddingley, sensible and dignified interpreter of the law, did something she hadn't done since she was a child. She acted entirely on impulse and without giving a thought to the consequences.

As Harry Koniski's tall visitor paused to look at his watch, she reached for the nearest object, which happened to be her discarded suit jacket, and dropped it out of the window.

It landed right at his feet.

The man stared down at it for a few seconds and then, very slowly, he raised his head. His eyes met her with a penetrating, very disconcerting perception that convinced her he guessed the sudden flight of her jacket was no accident.

'It's usual to drop handkerchiefs, I believe.' He spoke coldly, with a clipped disdain that made her squirm. 'Or have mating rituals changed since I was last in town?'

Angela gasped. 'I wasn't — I didn't . . . '

'Of course not. It just happened to slip out of your hand.'

'Yes, it did. I . . . ' No, it hadn't. She'd dropped that jacket on purpose to attract his attention. And she must have been out of her mind. Mating rituals indeed! 'I'm sorry,' she finished woodenly. 'I didn't mean to startle you.'

'You didn't.' He bent down, picked up the jacket and swung it on the end of one finger. 'I presume I'm supposed to carry this up your steps and hand it back with a bow?'

'No,' said Angela. 'Just leave it on the railing. I'll be right down.'

'That's precisely what I intended to do, Ms Baddingley. Good afternoon.' He nodded curtly, leaving her no chance to ask him how he knew her name, and loped nonchalantly off down the street.

By the time Angela reached the doorway, he was out of sight.

And good riddance, she thought, as

she picked up the offending jacket. How *could* I have been so stupid? It must be the heat. That and overwork — and the fact that I haven't been out with a man since my last holiday. Remembering that man, she made a face. He had seemed all right when she met him, at a ski lodge up in the Cascades, but he'd turned out to have a fetish about ears. Hers, apparently, were the wrong shape.

Angela, you do not need a man, she reminded herself firmly. You need a secretary, and it's time you did something about it. Getting Sarah to fill in when you're desperate is no solution.

'I know, I know.' She sank heavily into the chair behind her neatly organised desk and realised she was talking to herself. Again. It had to stop.

Adjusting her glasses, she switched on her computer and spent the rest of the afternoon resolutely concentrating on work and the ongoing problem of locating efficient office help. She knew that if she allowed her mind to stray for even a moment it was likely to return to that horrible, handsome man whose eyes had seen right through her juvenile attempt to attract his attention. And she didn't want to think about him. It was too embarrassing.

The next morning, when Angela arrived at her office, she found an unstamped letter in her mail box. It was from a Robin Bolan, who was applying for the position of secretary. There was no phone number on it, and no return address, but Miss Bolan announced that she would be calling on Ms Baddingley at ten.

Angela rolled up her eyes. Miss Bolan didn't appear to have much idea of correct business procedure. But lawyers in need of office help couldn't be choosers, and no one else had volunteered for the job. She would have to give the woman a chance.

At five to ten there was a sharp rap on her door, and before she had a chance to say, Come in, it was pushed open.

A lanky young man with a head of bright red curls stood in the doorway, his lower lip protruding pugnaciously.

'Good morning,' said Angela. 'Can I help you?'

'I'm Robin,' said the young man.

Angela blinked and brushed a strand of light brown hair off the front of her blouse. 'Robin Bolan?' she asked cautiously. '*You're* Robin Bolan?'

'Yup.'

'Oh. And you're applying for the position as my secretary?' She had to be sure this wasn't some ludicrous mistake.

'That's right.'

Well, if she hired him, this taciturn young person wasn't likely to distract her with chit-chat, she thought wryly. That was something. 'Can you type?' she asked, rather enjoying this surprising role reversal.

'Yup. And I make a mean cup of coffee.'

Angela smiled. 'Well that's a bonus. Would you like to fill out an application?'

Robin closed the door behind him and slouched against it with his hands in his pockets. 'Why? So you can find some reason not to hire me?'

Angela leaned back in her chair and took her glasses off. She often found it easier to be blunt when her vision was blurred. 'No, because I need more information than you've given me, and I prefer to have it in writing. I might add that if I wanted to turn you down, my friend, you've given me a number of excuses already. For one thing, if you scowl at my clients like that, you'll scare them away. Now, do you want to fill out a form or don't you?'

'OK.' He took the form she held out to him, and gave her something that might have been an apology for a smile.

Without much hope of solving her staffing problem, Angela put her glasses on again and added the finishing touches to a partnership contract while Robin filled out the form.

He handed it back to her much

sooner than she expected, and she was pleased to note that, if nothing else, the young man had legible writing. She also noted with some surprise that he had all the qualifications needed for the job, plus one month's experience with a law firm.

'Only one month?' she asked, looking up. 'Why did you leave?'

'I didn't. It was temporary.'

All right, that made sense. Angela went on reading, all the time conscious that there was a tension emanating from Robin Bolan as he stood scowling in front of her that didn't make much sense at all.

When she reached the bottom of the form she discovered the reason for his defensiveness.

Under 'Have you ever been convicted of a criminal offence?' he had written 'Yes.'

'Car theft?' she asked with a sigh.

'Yup. And B and E.'

She nodded. 'Breaking and entering. Anything else?'

He glanced at her sharply. 'That's not enough?'

'Enough for what?'

'Enough for you to refuse me the job.'

She shook her head. 'Not necessarily. I asked you if there was anything else.' Angela picked up a pen and tapped it sharply on the edge of her desk.

'No. That's it. I got a suspended sentence.'

'First offence?'

'Uh-huh.'

'Hmm.' She put the pen down and waved him to one of two black and chrome chairs beside her desk. 'Sit down, Mr Bolan.'

'You mean you might still hire me?' He sat down slowly, as if he suspected her of hot-wiring the seat.

'Maybe. Tell me — who told you I needed a secretary?'

'Mr Koniski.'

'Oh, you know Harry. That explains it. There's not much goes on around here that Harry Koniski doesn't know

12

more about sooner.'

Robin shook his head. 'Not that Mr Koniski. His son. Ryan.'

'His . . . ? Oh, yes. I did hear he had a son. There were some rumours . . . ' She stopped abruptly. Of course there were rumours. There always were in Caley Cove. Which didn't mean she paid them any attention.

Robin was vigorously nodding his head. 'That's him. He defended me in court, but he said if I got in trouble again he'd personally kick my butt all the way to Portland.'

Angela glanced at the application. 'Instead of which, he gave you a job in his office.'

'Yup, but only for a while. Then yesterday he phoned and told me you needed a secretary, and to get down here. Fast.'

'I see. You live in Port Angeles, do you?'

'Yup. But I can easily move. Ryan says I can stay with his dad and his aunt until I find my own place to live.'

'Yes.' Angela studied him thoughtfully over the top of her glasses. He was presentable enough, and engagingly forthright when he took the trouble to link more than two sentences together. 'And where is — um — Ryan Koniski now? Can I talk to him?'

Robin's face closed up like a slightly pink clam. 'You don't believe me.'

'Why shouldn't I believe you?' She flapped a hand at the application. 'Everything here is easy enough to verify. All the same, I'd like to talk to Mr Koniski.'

'He's with his dad. Shall I tell him you've gotta see him right away?'

'Yes, please. Although you might put it more tactfully than that.'

An hour later, as the sun continued to beat down on the roof, the door was pushed open again, and a tall man, jaw stiffened aggressively, strode across the floor to her desk. One look at his face was enough to tell Angela that in all probability her message had *not* been delivered tactfully, and that the man

14

with the icy grey eyes was not amused. Staring into those eyes now, she only just managed to suppress a groan.

She might have known. In fact she *ought* to have known.

Not only was her visitor unamused, he was also the man in blue denim who yesterday had failed to be even remotely diverted by an unexpected encounter with her jacket.

'You!' she exclaimed. What *were* those rumours she'd heard? Something about his past . . . She must try to find out. Not usually a problem in Caley Cove, she acknowledged ruefully.

'We meet again, Ms Baddingley,' her visitor was saying coolly. 'Rob tells me I've been summoned to a hearing.'

'Well, I . . . ' She swallowed. Why did he have this effect on her? She didn't normally stammer, and she was never tongue-tied. 'Mr Koniski,' she said, getting a firm grip on herself, 'I didn't summon you, as you put it. I asked Robin to tell you I'd like to see you.'

'OK.' He pressed his knuckles on to

her desk and leaned towards her. 'You're seeing me. Do I pass muster?'

Oh, he passed all right. Close up, he was mouth-wateringly gorgeous. Or he would have been if he didn't look so stern and austere. Yet in spite of that forbidding austerity there was an aura of tough, earthy virility about him that made her think he had to be more than just Robin's city-slicker lawyer. He even *smelled* male and compelling. If only . . .

'There's no muster to pass, Mr Koniski.' She pulled herself together with an effort, and replied with businesslike briskness.

He didn't answer at once, but instead allowed his gaze to flick down her face and over the soft swell of her breasts beneath the sensible office-issue white blouse.

She opened her mouth, intending to ask him about Robin but, incredibly, found herself saying instead, 'What about me, Mr Koniski? Do I pass?'

He straightened and crossed his arms

16

on his chest, smiling now, a full and disturbingly speculative smile. Then he put his head on one side and said deliberately, as if he were totting up the good points of a horse, 'Hmm. Neat, shoulder-length brown hair — I like brown — average height, good figure, pretty hazel eyes behind those glasses, peaches-and-cream skin, nice straight nose, lips — soft and probably kiss-able — '

'*Mr Koniski!*' Angela finally found her voice. 'I wasn't asking you — '

His smile stretched, became intentionally provoking. 'Weren't you? I could have sworn you were. In any case I'm not part of the bargain.'

'What bargain?' Angela gripped the leather arms of her chair.

Instead of answering directly, Ryan perched himself on a corner of her desk and said with a total lack of warmth, 'You wanted to see me so that you could explain to Harry Koniski's son that you couldn't possibly hire a young *man* — especially one with a record.

17

Isn't that so? Awkward for you, but easier than explaining to Rob's face. You figured that as a fellow upholder of the law I'd understand. Then you realised I was the man you'd set your sights on yesterday, and decided to alter the game plan.'

'What are you talking about?' Angela's nails began to dig into the leather. 'I hadn't made up my mind about Robin. I thought you might be able to shed some light on his background. And no, I *didn't* realise who you were until you came barging in here, but I've never had a game plan, and I'm damned if I see you as any bargain.'

'You're right there,' he said, with so much bitterness that Angela blinked.

'What do you mean?'

'It doesn't matter. Look . . . ' He stood up suddenly then flung himself down on one of her black and chrome chairs. 'Let's start over. Yesterday you made a pass at me. And maybe I'm crazy — after all, you're an attractive woman — but I make it my policy never to respond to passes. I prefer to make all my own moves. Also I can't stand game-playing. I see too much of it in my job. So I didn't pick up your gauntlet — '

'Actually it was a jacket,' said Angela, who couldn't believe this conversation was happening, but saw no reason to pretend that Ryan wasn't right. He was obviously an arrogant, thoroughly conceited reptile, but she *had* been making a pass at him, albeit without premeditation. It had been a mistake, and she didn't like game-playing either.

To her surprise, Ryan's lips twitched briefly. 'That's better,' he said. 'As long as you understand that Rob has to get this job on his own merits, or not at all.'

'Dear me,' said Angela, suddenly determined to turn the tables on this over-confident, much too complacent man. 'Do you mean you're not putting up your body as part of the package? It's a very nice one, of course, but now that I see it up close I'm not sure it's quite — well, you know.' She pursed her lips — the ones he'd said were 'probably kissable' — and added judiciously, 'A nice bit of beefcake, mind you, but not — no, I really don't think so. Don't worry, Mr Koniski. On balance, I'm not tempted to request that sort of collateral.'

Angela had the enormous satisfaction of watching Ryan Koniski's jaw drop. But only for an instant. The next moment his tawny-gold head was thrown back as he let out a crack of reluctant laughter. It was a nice laugh, she reflected dazedly, even if it didn't last long. Deep, and appealingly sexy.

'Round two to you,' he conceded, sobering quickly. 'Listen, Ms Baddingley, we've obviously got off on the wrong foot. I'm sure you see me as a vain and self-satisfied chauvinist. Which normally wouldn't worry me in the least — '

'I didn't think it would,' said Angela.

'Really?' He crossed his legs and looked her impassively in the eye. 'Then you'd be right. But I hope your feelings towards me won't influence your decision about Rob. Why *did* you want to see me, dare I ask?'

'I didn't want to see you. At least I did, but I didn't know you were you. Robin — Rob — said that you were the one who suggested he apply for the job, and I need to know why you think a young man who's been convicted of petty crime is likely to be an asset around a law office.' She adjusted her glasses. 'My clients take a dim view of theft, Mr Koniski, and I don't want them to feel they have to check their pockets every time they need to see their lawyer.'

'I see.' His face was inscrutable now, blank as a page from an unwritten book. But Angela had a sense that behind the enigmatic façade he was seething.

'Do you?' she asked doubtfully.

'I think so. You're the sort who believes that once a crime has been committed the perpetrator should be permanently branded. You pay lip-service to the idea of reform, but you

21

have no faith in it. Someone like Rob, who with a bit of support and the occasional kick in the pants has every hope of becoming a useful citizen, has about as much chance as a mosquito in your books.'

Angela experienced a wave of fury the like of which she hadn't known since the day Kelvin tried to make her leave law school. 'Now you listen to me,' she snapped, standing up and placing both hands flat on her desk to prevent herself from placing them round his neck. 'Don't start blaming me because your Rob decided to steal cars and break into some innocent victim's happy home — '

'I wasn't blaming you.'

'Yes, you were. I believe that people can turn themselves around just as strongly as you do. The truth, though, is that a great many don't. I want to know why you think Rob is the exception.' She knew she must look like an angry hen defending its nest, but she couldn't help herself. Ryan Koniski was just about the most irritating and offensive man she had ever met. Unfortunately, he also came close to being the sexiest.

'OK,' he said, swivelling the black chair sideways, and adding insult to injury by linking long arms behind his neck and studying the ceiling instead of her. 'I won't bore you with the details of Rob's neglected childhood, or how he came under the influence of the wrong friends. Hardly your problem, I agree. However, I will say that his trial and subsequent suspended sentence appear to have brought him up short. He worked for a month in my office as secretary to my partner, and we were pleasantly surprised at how well he made out. Even took all the kidding about his lack of blonde hair and sexy curves in good part — '

'If he's such a paragon, why isn't your firm keeping him on, then?' demanded Angela.

'Because the young lady he was filling in for has returned from her leave of absence, and we can't employ every reformed delinquent I happen to defend.'

'Oh. So you think — '

'I think that given half a chance there is every likelihood that Rob will do as good a job for you as he did for Martin.'

Lord, it was hot in here. Angela pushed her hair back and sat down again, her anger dissipated. Ryan obviously felt strongly about his protégé, and, although she had no reason to trust his judgement, surely it wouldn't be in his own best interest to talk her into employing a deadbeat? Word would get round, and it would do nothing for his firm's credibility.

'At least he wouldn't leave to raise a family,' she muttered, more to herself than to him.

'What?' Ryan swung himself back to face her. 'Is that remark as blatantly sexist as it sounds?'

'In reverse? Yes, I suppose it is,' admitted Angela. 'And if you're about to tell me I ought to be ashamed of myself — '

'It crossed my mind.'

'I'll bet. And I hate to admit it, but you're right.' She hesitated, studied his impassive face through her eyelashes. 'Very well, Mr Koniski, you're on. Or rather Rob is.'

'Just like that?' A slow smile spread across his face. It made him look younger, less formidable, and without meaning to Angela found herself smiling cautiously back.

She shook her head. 'No, not just like that. I'll give him a month's trial, though, and if he proves satisfactory I'll keep him on.'

'You surprise me, Ms Baddingley.'

'Why? Because I didn't turn out to be some biased, complacent dragon lady who believes in locking people up and losing keys?'

This time it was Ryan who stood up and placed both hands flat on the desk. 'If you must know, yes. That's exactly why.'

Well, he was honest anyway. So far it was the most positive quality he'd exhibited. But there was something in his voice which puzzled her. Something dark and strained that made her feel uneasy. 'I'm not like that at all,' she said quickly. When he continued to gaze down at her as if she hadn't spoken, she felt compelled to add, 'But the truth is, I badly need a secretary. If Rob is as useful as you say he is, I have no choice but to hire him.'

'And if you had a choice?' He wasn't smiling now, and his tone was cold.

'Don't push me, Mr Koniski. You've got what you came for.'

'Not quite.'

'What do you mean?' All of a sudden Angela felt a liquid sensation somewhere below her knees, and she was glad she was sitting down because Ryan's eyes were having an unfortunate effect on her breathing.

'You said you didn't require any collateral to seal the bargain,' he replied with no emphasis whatever.

'No, of course I don't,' she said hastily. 'Not that sort of collateral anyway.'

'And what sort would that be?'

'Well, I don't want ... ' She hesitated, searching for a phrase that would leave him in no doubt that the incident with the jacket had been nothing more than an innocent blunder.

'Me?' he suggested, as if he were discussing her preference in toothpaste. 'You've made that quite clear, Ms Baddingley. But it occurs to me that there may be a problem. What if Rob proves satisfactory, but someone young and female with a clean record turns up before the end of the month? You must see that I need some assurance you won't dismiss him without cause. Something to seal the bargain, shall we say?'

Angela gaped up at him, speechless. When he held out his hand, though, she took it, and allowed him to pull her slowly to her feet.

2

Ryan's fingers tightened over Angela's palm. He wondered if she knew how lovely she was once she dropped the strictly-business façade she'd been adopting to keep him at arm's length. When her guard was down, as it was now, she looked like a shy young girl waiting for her lover. Those big hazel eyes behind the glasses were as wide and anxious as a doe's. A confused doe, though, who wasn't sure if he was predator or friend. Strange that, because up until now she had come across as an unusually strong and independent lady who would give any hunter back as good as, or better than, she got.

He watched a faint blush of rose touch her cheeks, and wondered if he wanted to hunt this unexpectedly available prey. Once, he wouldn't have hesitated. But that was a long time ago, before he'd learned to avoid all but the most casual relationships — and those infrequently. There was something about this woman, though, that wasn't casual. Which was odd, because it was obvious she expected him to kiss her, and she didn't strike him as the kiss-on-first-meeting type.

No. He made up his mind. It wouldn't be fair to her. She was too damn desirable, it had been too long since he'd held a woman in his arms, and he wasn't about to start something he couldn't stop. Not in this God-forsaken town whose biting tongues could so easily destroy a reputation. He couldn't — wouldn't — inflict that on this spunky, yet strangely vulnerable lady.

He swallowed the sudden taste of bile in his mouth, turned over her hand and dropped a light kiss on her knuckles.

'What are you doing?' Angela managed to hang on to a pale remnant of her normal composure as she felt her heart race in a manner she considered more suited to the flutterings of a romantic schoolgirl than to a sober and successfully divorced solicitor. 'What do you want?'

'I told you. Some assurance that you won't dismiss Rob without cause.' His gaze took in the quick rise and fall of her chest, then fastened on the soft outline of her mouth. 'And I think I have that assurance,' he added calmly. 'Or at least a fair guarantee that if Rob runs into trouble not of his own making I'll have a certain degree of influence with his boss. Thank you, Ms Baddingley. That's good to know.'

Angela gaped at him. 'What are you talking about? I haven't — '

'Made any promises of a compromising nature? No, of course you haven't. That would be most unprofessional.'

'Yes, it certainly would. And I assure you I'm not interested — '

'OK. I'll take your word for it.' He interrupted her with an abruptness that convinced her he was anxious to bring their meeting to a close. 'I assume you want Rob to start tomorrow?'

'Yes.' Angela squared her shoulders. 'Nine o'clock.'

'Fine. I'll see he gets here. Goodbye, Ms Baddingley, and thank you — for Rob's sake.'

It was only when he shook her hand briefly and then released it that she realised he had been holding it all along, and that she'd liked the firm feel of his fingers on her skin. But by the time she'd recovered her senses he had let himself out and was already on his way down the stairs.

Angela stared after him. Of all the arrogant, self-satisfied . . . A certain degree of influence indeed! What did he mean by that? That if it suited him all he had to do was lift a finger and she'd come running? And did he really imagine she would let him tell her how to run her office? If he did, he had another think coming. In fact she had half a mind to change her mind about Robin — or Rob, as he was apparently called. Except that it wouldn't be fair to hold the young man responsible for the sins of his mentor.

She slapped a hand irritably on her desk, and then gazed down at it in vague surprise. It was the same hand Ryan Koniski had held on to for a shade too long, and it still felt warm. Frowning, she hurried into the bathroom and began to run cold water into the sink.

⋆   ⋆   ⋆

'Bye, Ms Baddingley. See ya tomorrow.'

'Bye, Rob. See you.' Angela watched the bright hair disappear through the doorway, and thought what a stroke of fortune the young man's arrival had been for the offices of A.P. Baddingley, Attorney. Fortune and Ryan Koniski.

In the month that Rob had been with her, he had proved wonderfully efficient and good-humoured. He was still a man of few words, but his taciturnity alternately amused or delighted her clients, who were generally more interested in their legal problems than in social chatter. Just yesterday, she had told him the job was his for as long as he wanted it.

Of Ryan she had seen nothing. Rob, who was boarding with Harry Koniski and his sister, Charlotte, told her he had returned to his practice in Seattle. But when she had tried to find out more from the normally loquacious inhabitants of Caley Cove — such as where he had been hiding out during the almost eleven years she had lived here, and the exact nature of the rumours about his past — she had been answered with shrugs, and the suggestion that she'd better ask him. Angela was left with the definite impression that Ryan wasn't popular in this town, but that people weren't talking.

Odd, she thought. Everybody talks about everything around here, and Harry Koniski is the source of at least half the gossip that comes around. If people aren't talking about his son, and they obviously aren't, there has to be a good reason. And yet, when she had first arrived, she was sure she'd heard something — something quickly suppressed about a wayward boy who had brought shame on his town. She wished she could remember . . .

Not that it was any of her business, she felt obliged to remind herself on occasion, especially as Ryan wasn't her favourite person. He had provided her with Rob, for which she was eternally grateful, but if she never saw the younger Koniski again it would be too soon.

To her chagrin, 'never' was the following afternoon.

In the morning Charlotte Koniski, Ryan's aunt, called from Harry's office to say that she'd found her brother collapsed on his desk, and could Angela please come . . .

Hearing the note of panic in Charlotte's voice, Angela didn't wait to hear more, but dashed across the road, sending a shower of contracts to the floor in her wake.

By the time she reached her old friend's office, Harry was sitting up looking dazed, his shock of white hair tumbled across his forehead. Charlotte, looking frightened, was trying to fan him with a scrawny potted plant. Angela gently removed the plant and phoned for help.

Fifteen minutes later an ambulance was bearing Harry and Charlotte to the hospital, and Angela was reluctantly lifting the phone to call Ryan. To her relief, he wasn't in his office, and all she could do was leave a succinct message with his partner.

She returned to her own office and tried unsuccessfully to concentrate on Frank Farraday's new will.

Eventually Charlotte called to say that Harry had had a heart attack but would recover. Then late in the afternoon, just as Frank was leaving her office, Angela looked up to see Ryan striding through the door like a one-man army on the march. Unable to halt his momentum, he almost knocked her client to the floor.

'My apologies,' said Ryan brusquely as he grasped Frank's elbow to steady him. 'No serious damage done, I hope?'

'No thanks to you.' Frank gave him a disgusted look and departed in what looked like a huff.

Angela stared at Ryan silently, taking in the dark grey business suit which made him look even more pressed, severe and remote than she remembered. In spite of the continuing heat, he seemed cool. But his forbidding appearance didn't stop her stomach doing an irritating cartwheel.

'Sorry,' said Ryan, still curt. 'I didn't come here to drive away your business.'

'You won't. I'm the only attorney in town. Unless *you're* planning on setting up shop here?'

His mouth turned down at one corner. 'Not a chance. I'm about as popular as your average cockroach in Caley Cove.'

'Why's that?' asked Angela, who had

formed precisely the same impression herself.

'It's not important.'

'Then why mention it?' Angela was irritated by his brusqueness but still curious.

He shrugged. 'Habit.'

'What's that supposed to mean?'

'Nothing that need concern you.' He picked up a pen and began to tap it on the edge of her desk.

Angela took one look at the harsh line of his mouth, removed the pen from his fingers and said, 'Why are you here?'

His mouth softened marginally, and he said in a voice that was suddenly much warmer, 'I came to thank you for what you did for my father. Aunt Charlotte says she'd never have managed without you.'

Angela nodded coolly. 'I happened to be the one Charlotte called. It was nothing.'

'It was to Aunt Charlotte.' She saw the muscles in his neck contract slightly, and had an idea he was having trouble getting words out. 'And to me.'

'My pleasure,' said Angela gravely, wishing it weren't, quite literally, true. She did feel an absurd little thrill of pleasure that he was grateful. And it was ridiculous. This man was giving her the kind of ideas she hadn't entertained since her divorce. Oh, she hadn't been totally celibate, of course, but there had been no serious passion, and only one liaison that had amounted to more than a brief holiday romance. And even that had eventually been cancelled due to lack of interest. On both sides.

The day her marriage broke up she had vowed to guard her freedom as a precious gift, and she had had no difficulty keeping that vow. Of course her success in her chosen profession had helped. Everyone had told her she was too young to strike out alone after only a short time with a law firm. And everyone had been wrong. She had done well, and she was proud of her success. It made her single bliss taste that much better.

So why, now, was she eyeing this cold powerhouse of a man as if he could give her something she lacked?

'Rob is working out very well,' she said abruptly, because Ryan was frowning at her as if he too suspected he was missing something — something he didn't particularly want.

'Good.' His frown deepened, and Angela waited for some critical pronouncement. But all he said was, 'Thank you again, Ms Baddingley,' before he spun round and strode out of her office. The next thing she knew, he was on his way down the stairs, taking them three steps at a time.

'Hey,' she shouted after him. 'Don't forget to let me know how your father is. Or if there's anything I can do to help.'

'You can't help,' he shouted back.

'Well, anyway, do let me know.'

The only answer she received was the slam of the door as he headed out into the street.

'Rude reptile,' she muttered, making for the window. 'It wouldn't have hurt him to say goodbye politely.'

Ryan was already swinging a long leg through the door of a sleek white Alfa-Romeo. As she watched, he settled into the seat, started up the engine and disappeared in a cloud of summer dust.

'And I hope it ruins that power suit of yours,' she yelled at the hot and unresponsive street.

Only a fat white cat wallowing in the shade of a plum tree paid her any attention — and he only flicked his tail and went back to sleep. Angela reminded herself that Ryan was probably anxious about his father, and tried not to dream of committing violence against his very delectable person. Violence interspersed with rampaging sex.

She gazed glumly at the heat haze hovering over the peaks of the Olympics, wiped a thin film of perspiration off her forehead, and began to tidy her already orderly desk.

Four hours later, dressed in blue denim shorts and a pink vest-top, she was reclining on her back patio high above the Strait of Juan de Fuca while she consumed a sinfully comforting bowl of strawberries drowned in thick cream. Which, she acknowledged ruefully, would probably put paid to any benefits her body might have gained from the half-hour she had spent exercising that morning.

A small grey bird with a dull red breast and a dilapidated crest was perched on her shoulder eyeing the repast with beady anticipation.

The doorbell rang just as she put down the bowl.

'Grack,' said the bird disgustedly.

'I know, I know,' Angela replied. 'I heard it too.' She stood up. Who could be calling on her at this hour? She wasn't expecting company, and her isolated, ranch-style bungalow at the end of a dusty gravel road was usually sufficiently far out of town to discourage casual droppers-in.

Probably an over-zealous salesman, she decided, glancing through the peephole before she pulled open the door.

But it wasn't a salesman. Incomprehensibly, it was Ryan.

He rang the bell again, impatiently, and Angela closed her mouth and let him in.

He looked considerably more rumpled than when he had called in at her office. The top button of his shirt was undone, he had discarded his tie, and his tawny hair was attractively dishevelled. Angela groaned inwardly. The man was impossible. He had no right to look seductive in everything from boardroom suits to jeans — with all the enticing permutations in between.

'What is it?' she asked, controlling a startling urge to smooth his hair. 'Is your father all right?'

'Yes. He's fine. That's what I came to tell you.' His gaze swept over her scantily clad figure, and swept away again, as if she were swathed in a burnous.

'Oh. Thank you. You didn't need to

— I mean, you could have phoned.'

'I know. I chose not to. If you must know, I was glad of the excuse to escape from Aunt Charlotte's nurturing clutches. She has all systems switched on to 'fuss'. They wouldn't let her stay at the hospital, Rob had the good sense to be out, and that left me as the only target for her ministrations. When Clara Malone came over to commiserate, I took advantage of the chance to slip away.'

'I'm glad I provided an excuse for you,' said Angela, who wasn't glad, and felt quite unreasonably resentful. 'So aren't you going to tell me about your father?'

'I already have. With luck he'll be home in a few days — for which I'm almost as thankful as he is. The sooner he recovers, the sooner I can get back to civilisation.'

'Caley Cove isn't uncivilised.'

'I suppose not, if the jungle telegraph is your idea of cultured communication.' When he saw Angela's mouth open to protest, he added smoothly, 'So aren't you going to tell me why you have that moth-eaten fowl on your shoulder?'

'Al's not moth-eaten. He's just a bit — wilted. He's my cockatiel, and he lives here.'

'OK, if you say so. Next question. Are you going to invite me in for a drink?'

It wasn't really a question, Angela noted. This was a man who expected to get what he wanted.

'Lemonade?' she asked, suspecting he meant something stronger.

'That'll do.'

He sounded worn out, and when Angela took a closer look at his face she saw that there were deep lines of fatigue around his eyes. Taking pity on him, she admitted, 'I do have whisky somewhere if you prefer it.'

'Provided 'somewhere' is reasonably accessible, I do prefer it.'

'As a matter of fact I think it's in the septic tank,' she replied cheerfully — and was a little disappointed to see him grin.

When he followed her into her spotless white kitchen, she told him to help himself to the whisky — which turned up at the back of a cupboard — while she poured herself a small glass of wine.

As soon as they were settled in Cape Cod chairs on the patio — with Al still clinging to her shoulder — Angela said, 'All right, now tell me. Did you really come all this way just to thank me? Outside of wanting to get away from Charlotte?'

The grey eyes glanced at her sharply. 'What else would I come for?' He rested an ankle on his knee and leaned back, nursing his glass. 'All right, I suppose I also came to apologise for my rude response to your offer of help.'

'It's OK. You were worried.'

'Yes. But not as worried as poor Aunt Charlotte. I haven't seen her so upset since . . . ' He stopped abruptly.

'Since . . . ?' Angela prodded.

'It doesn't matter.' He scowled into his drink.

Angela sighed. He really was an impossibly reticent man. 'You left home a long time ago, didn't you?' she asked, hoping to learn something that way.

She had often read of shadows crossing people's faces, and hadn't believed it meant anything till now. But there was no other description for the way Ryan's features suddenly seemed to cloud over and turn dark.

'Twenty,' he said shortly. And then, as if the words were being dragged out of him, 'Aunt Charlotte brought me up.'

Angela frowned at him, puzzled. Why did that innocuous statement sound so loaded with meaning?

'Your mother . . . ?' she murmured, trying to remember what she'd heard about Harry's wife.

Ryan lifted his head, so that the evening sun emphasised the hard angles of his face. 'She died having me.'

There didn't seem much point in saying, 'I'm sorry,' after all these years, but she said it anyway.

His smile was cynical. 'No reason why you should be.'

'No, but it must have been devastating for your father — and sad for you . . .'

'Right on both counts. Although I can't complain I was neglected. Shall we change the subject? What about you, Ms Baddingley? Do you have shadows in your past too, or have you always lived in affluent security?'

'Affluent?' exclaimed Angela. 'No, my father owns a small grocery store in Tacoma. Secure enough, I suppose, but my sister and I were expected to help out on weekends. We didn't get to take anything for granted.'

She didn't realise her voice had risen until Ryan lifted a sardonic eyebrow and said, 'I don't remember implying that you did. You do, however, have an attractive modern house with some good furniture, and a well-kept garden with an excellent view of the strait. Not an atmosphere conducive to shadows.'

Angela frowned. He almost made it

sound as though she was some sort of social parasite just because she'd worked hard enough to buy herself a house and a few nice things.

'Will an ordinary and fairly civilised divorce raise me in your estimation?' she asked, tapping her foot rapidly on the flagstones. 'Or doesn't that count as a shadow?'

'That depends,' he replied, looking more amused than disconcerted.

'On what?'

'On how you feel about it yourself.'

'I feel great about it,' snapped Angela.

'Then it doesn't count.'

'Grack,' said Al, and started to nibble on her ear.

'Oh, shut up, Al. Come on, it's time for a nap.' Irritated, but not with her pet, she stood up and carried the disgruntled bird back to his cage on a teak table in the corner of her living-room.

She knew Ryan was watching her through the glass doors as she slipped

Al on to his perch and fastened the door, but when she returned to the patio and threw herself back in her chair she wasn't prepared for the cutting contempt that blazed at her out of his eyes.

'What's the matter now?' she asked. 'Have I committed the unpardonable offence of admitting that I actually enjoy my life? Or is it something else? Like the fact that I haven't fallen for your debatable charms.'

'Haven't you? I thought you had.' He swallowed the remains of his drink and put the glass down carefully on her white metal patio table. 'But I'm relieved to hear I was wrong. I'm not in the business of charming lovely young lawyers.'

Angela stared at a cluster of deep red roses, their heads bobbing gently in the warm breeze blowing up off the water. 'I've noticed you don't go in for charm,' she muttered, suspecting she sounded like a child trying to have the last word. She knew Ryan was about to leave, and she still didn't know what she'd done to make him look at her as if she were a particularly loathsome species of slug.

'You're not going to tell me what's the matter, are you?' she said, twirling the stem of her wine glass.

'Nothing is.' He stood up, and again the darkness dropped across his face.

'Baloney!'

Ryan smiled, a flat, unaccommodating smile. 'You don't mince words, do you? Neither do I. All right, Ms Baddingley, the fact is I have no use for people who put helpless creatures in cages for their own amusement.'

'You mean Al?' Angela stood up and placed both hands on her hips. 'For your information, *Mr* Koniski, if I allowed Al total freedom, he'd die. He's had his wings clipped.'

'And you think having his wings clipped makes everything all right?' The scorn in his voice made Angela want to slap his handsome face.

'No, it does not make everything right,' she told him, gritting her teeth. 'However, *I'm* not the one who had it done. I got him from an animal shelter. Nobody else wanted to take him.'

'Hmm.'

She saw that Ryan finally had the grace to look contrite — or as contrite as she imagined he ever got — and she couldn't resist pressing her advantage. 'Apart from which, I don't see what it has to do with you.'

He took a handkerchief out of his pocket and wiped it round the back of his neck. 'Neither do I. I'm sorry.'

'It doesn't matter,' said Angela reluctantly. 'Just don't let it happen again.'

His lip tipped up at one corner in that way she found so maddeningly attractive. 'No danger of that,' he assured her.

'Oh?' Angela was unconvinced. 'Why's that?'

He shrugged. 'Because I rarely make the same mistake twice.'

When he turned away from her and took a half-step in the direction of the house, Angela laid a hand on his sleeve to detain him. 'Wait. What do you mean by that?' she demanded. 'What mistake?'

Ryan paused to glance down at the hand resting on the smooth fabric of his jacket, and when for a second he raised his eyes she wondered if he was as acutely aware of her as she was of him.

Up until this moment she had been certain he regarded her as just some crazy female who threw her clothes out of windows at passing hunks who happened to take her fancy. A crazy female who had her uses in the youth employment department, but was none the less barmy for that.

Now, very deliberately, he placed his hand over hers and left it there just long enough for her to feel the heat from it sizzling up her arm. Then, equally deliberately, he unclasped her fingers and moved away.

'You,' he replied, continuing his progress to the door.

'Me? Are you calling me a mistake?' Angela glared at his retreating back and looked round for a suitable missile — until she recalled that she was too old, and too sensible, to throw things.

'I'm not calling you anything,' he answered over his shoulder. 'Although I suspect you could very well become one of my major lapses. Which is why I'd suggest that if you know what's good for you, Ms Baddingley, you'll stay the hell out of my way. Goodbye, and thank you for the drink.'

'Hey,' Angela shouted after him. 'You can't just walk out on me like that. And how dare you accuse me of getting in your way? I didn't invite you to come here, you came of your own free will. And don't bother coming again.' He had already disappeared, so she hurried after him.

Ryan stopped halfway down the gravelled pathway. 'I can just walk out like that,' he said, facing her. 'I have. But you're right. You didn't invite me to come here, and I promise I won't do it again. Will that do?'

'Do for what?'

'An apology.' He smiled, a sensuous, appealing smile this time, and Angela's beleaguered stomach did another cart-wheel.

'It will have to, won't it?' she said grumpily, and went back into the house. The crash of the door slamming behind her jarred all her nerve-ends and didn't do a thing to restore her humour.

'Damn him,' she muttered to Al, as she lifted the little bird out of his cage. 'Ryan Koniski is without a doubt the rudest, most obnoxious man I have ever met, and yet there's something about him . . . Underneath that gorgeously abrasive exterior I can't help thinking there's a human being wanting to get out.'

'Grack,' said Al helpfully, cocking his head to one side.

Angela stroked his feathers. 'I know. He's certainly on your side, isn't he? Funny that. I wonder why he feels so strongly?'

When Al chose not to answer, she

went on thoughtfully, 'He went to bat for Rob too when there was no special reason why he should. All the same . . . ' she took a deep breath ' . . . there's no doubt he's a bastard. If only he weren't so damned attractive . . . '

As Angela picked up the empty bowl that had contained her strawberries, she forced herself to remember that Ryan had assured her he wasn't coming back. There was no reason to think he would arrive on her doorstep to shatter her comfortable stability again. Once his father recovered, he'd be on his way back to Seattle. So the fact that he was attractive didn't matter.

She dumped the bowl into the sink, pensively demolished four ginger chocolates she'd been saving for tomorrow, and wondered why the thought of Ryan's departure didn't give her nearly as much satisfaction as it should.

Three days later Rob informed her that Harry was home and itching to get back to work.

'Oh,' said Angela. 'I suppose that means Ryan will be leaving.'

'Tomorrow morning,' Rob grunted.

She drew in the corner of her lip, smoothed her skirt and said inanely, 'How nice.' When her assistant looked at her as if he suspected she was losing her grip, she remembered that she was supposed to be a level-headed business-woman, and began to search busily for a file she hadn't lost.

The following evening after supper, she picked up a selection of the mystery novels she knew Harry loved, and went to call on the Koniskis.

The older, two-storey brick house on Caley Cove's longest established street looked deserted when Angela arrived. The curtains were half drawn and Harry's white station wagon was absent from the open garage. But she climbed the steps anyway and knocked.

There was no answer, which didn't surprise her, so she looked round for somewhere to leave the books. The step wouldn't do. A small boy with a jam-covered face and fingers was peering at her over the fence, and she knew curiosity would get the better of both him and the books if she left them where he could get at them.

'Hopeless,' she muttered, rejecting a drainpipe and a Japanese maple beside the door.

'What's hopeless?' enquired a voice from behind her.

Angela jumped and dropped *Fingers of Death* and *The Bloodstained Hand* on the concrete.

'Let me,' said the voice as, automatically, she bent to pick them up. The next moment a powerful forearm was extended over her shoulder and the books were swept up out of sight.

Angela gulped and straightened quickly. There was no mistaking that voice.

Sure enough, when she turned round, it was to find herself standing almost chest to chest with Ryan Koniski. She could feel his warm breath stroking her cheek.

3

'Ryan,' she murmured, knowing she ought to move, but unaccountably frozen to the step. 'What are you — ? I mean, you're not here. You're in Seattle.'

His hypnotic eyes glinted silver with what might have been amusement. 'I assure you, I'm not a mirage. Flesh and blood right to the bone.'

She didn't need him to tell her that. The intense stimulation of that flesh and blood, exuding its own kind of alchemy, was causing her legs to turn into cotton — and her mind to forget everything except the excruciating torture of a desire so strong she was tempted to fling her arms around him and give the neighbours an exhibition they would be talking about for years. But somehow, although she couldn't quite manage to move away from him, she succeeded in keeping her hands stiffly at her sides.

'I didn't hear your car,' she said, as though that weren't as obvious as the pink flush tinting her cheeks. She hadn't either. It was parked at the kerb, but she had been so absorbed with finding a safe place for the books that she hadn't even heard it pull up.

'Riny!' shouted the jam-faced child from next door. 'Riny wanna play?'

Ryan, who had been gazing at her with a slight lift of his eyebrows, gave the small neighbour a friendly wave and shook his head. ''Fraid not, Billy. How about tomorrow? Early.'

Billy kicked at the fence and muttered a reluctant, 'OK.'

Ryan's eyes met Angela's again. 'No inhibiting pink glasses today?' he asked lightly. 'Does that mean you can't actually see me?'

'Of course I can. Contacts. I only use my glasses for work.' Angela spoke curtly, annoyed that he had called her glasses inhibiting.

'I see,' he drawled. 'So the hard-boiled attorney act is mostly a disguise. I thought it might be. Would you like to come in?'

He didn't sound as if he intended her to accept, and Angela was about to say no when he raised an arm and brushed his fingers carelessly through his hair. The movement tightened the muscles beneath his dark blue T-shirt, and a faint, very masculine scent tantalised the lining of her nose.

'Yes. Thank you,' she replied, unfastening the top button of her pale green shirt. Then, realising what she was doing, she fumbled frantically to do it up again.

Ryan watched her in silence, but when her efforts only succeeded in releasing the next button he reached over and slipped both of them smartly back into place.

'A tempting offer,' he said. 'But I don't think so.'

'Oh! I wasn't — '

'Of course you weren't.' He put his

hands on her waist, moved her to the side and, inserting a key in the lock, swung open the heavy panelled door.

'After you.' He gestured at the hallway.

Angela's eyes dropped, and she took in for the first time that he was wearing cut-offs. She might have known he'd have legs to kill for. She groaned inwardly and stifled a laugh which, if she permitted it to escape, she knew would come out like a bad case of hysterics.

Ryan was gazing at her with his eyebrows arched, so she took a deep breath and marched past him into the house.

'It's warm out,' she murmured, as he took her arm and led her into a living-room with bright yellow walls and a surprising collection of furniture that looked as if it had been assembled for the express purpose of opening a second-hand junk shop. The inside of the Koniski house was a source of never-ending amazement to Angela.

Harry was incapable of passing up an auction, and Charlotte admitted quite cheerfully that she was incapable of throwing anything out. The result, as Rob had remarked with a chuckle, was an ever-changing obstacle course.

'Yes,' agreed Ryan, watching her negotiate two sets of bellows and a stuffed tiger. 'It is, indeed, warm out. But you didn't drive all the way over here to tell me that.'

'No, I came to see how your father was doing. And to bring him the books. I thought you'd gone back to Seattle.'

'So you said. I haven't. To the delight of Mrs Rainbow, who is busy summer-cleaning my apartment.'

'So I see.' Angela sat down on an orange plastic hassock shaped like an ailing mushroom, and wondered what in the world she was doing here. Harry was mysteriously out, and the last time she had seen Ryan he had made it very clear that he wasn't interested in keeping up their acquaintance. She stood up again and said hurriedly,

'Well, since Harry isn't here — '

Surprisingly, Ryan smiled. 'He couldn't stand the inactivity. He was giving poor Aunt Charlotte such a bad time that she finally agreed to take him out for a drive. He's convinced he must have missed something in the few days he hasn't been around to keep tabs.' He sighed heavily. 'Not being addicted to lengthy discussions of who isn't sleeping with whom, and why not, I opted to drive Rob to the dentist instead of joining the investigative party.'

Angela grinned, relieved to hear that Harry was well on the road to recovery and back on the trail of Caley Cove's latest scandals.

'I'm surprised at you,' she reproved Ryan. 'Turning down an opportunity like that.'

'Like what?' he asked, frowning.

'The perfect chance for father-son bonding.' She smiled artlessly, hoping her comment would induce him to throw some light on the mystery of his long absence from Caley Cove.

It didn't.

He shook his head and flung himself into a red fake-leather recliner that clashed outrageously with the mushroom. 'Father-son combat, you mean. Dad will enjoy himself much better without me. My presence tends to put a damper on gossip.'

'Oh,' said Angela, wondering if this was her chance to find out about the rumours without, in any way, upsetting Harry. 'I think I did hear you had some problem — '

'Yes.' Ryan cut her off so harshly that she jumped. 'You surely did. And now you're hoping to hear more, I suppose.'

'No, of course not.' Angela adjusted the waistband of her fawn-coloured skirt and began to edge her way towards the door. But Ryan was lying back in the recliner now, and although his face was grim his long legs were stretched enticingly in front of him. She moistened her lips, suddenly bowled over by a searing physical need the like of which she hadn't known for years.

That, combined with a strong desire to know more about this enigmatic man who had shaken her to her comfortable foundations, made her pause to ask him quickly, 'Why does it? Put a damper, I mean. Why have you stayed away for so long?'

For a moment she thought he would refuse to answer. Although his eyes expressed no emotion, his lips flattened and his jaw began to remind her of a rock. But in the end he said without altering the harsh pitch of his voice, 'My father and I had a disagreement. I caused him a great deal of grief, for which Caley Cove hasn't forgiven me. This town has a long memory, Ms Baddingley. Does that satisfy your curiosity?'

'Angela,' she said, not quite steadily. 'My name's Angela.' And no, it didn't satisfy her curiosity, but she could see that Ryan wasn't nearly as indifferent as he sounded. The veins in his neck and forearms stood out as if they'd been twisted from within. And she found herself wanting to run to him, to put her arms around him and smooth the lines of strain from between his brows.

Instead she moved the hassock up beside him, sat down again, and repeated, 'Angela. Not Ms Baddingley. Please.'

She kept her gaze fixed firmly on a delicate Japanese print hanging above a grinning ebony mask, and eventually she heard Ryan utter a sound that might have been a laugh, but probably wasn't.

'Angela,' he repeated. 'Angel. It's a pretty name. And are you an angel of the ministering persuasion?'

'Not usually.'

This time it was definitely a laugh, albeit a cracked one. 'I didn't think so.'

'Do you need ministering to?' she asked, still with her gaze on the print. When he didn't answer, she went on in a rush, 'Why should Caley Cove care about an ancient disagreement with your father? It's nobody's business.'

'My dear Ms — Angela. You've lived

here for almost eleven years. Surely by now you know better than to ask a question like that.'

'I should, shouldn't I?' She turned to smile up at him quite naturally. 'I guess what I really meant was that it wasn't *my* business. I'm sorry I asked.'

'No need to be. I wouldn't have answered you unless I chose to.' He picked up a strand of her hair and ran it with seeming abstraction through his fingers. 'You have beautiful hair, Angela, do you know that? Smooth and strokable — like silk.'

'I . . . ' She swallowed, unable to answer coherently. To the best of her knowledge, it was the first real compliment he had paid her, and it made her feel as inarticulate as a bashful young girl — which she hadn't been for longer than she cared to remember.

'It's all right,' he said, as if he understood her confusion. 'That wasn't a prelude to a pass. Just a way of avoiding explanations.'

'You don't owe me any explanations,'

said Angela, who was well aware that she half wished it *had* been a pass. 'I asked a question, you answered it, that's all.'

'I didn't answer it. Not fully.'

Angela frowned. He was still drawing her hair through his fingers. 'Oh. Wasn't it true, then that — ?'

'That I had a disagreement with my father? Yes, that was true enough. It kept me away from Caley Cove for twenty years.' His voice was even, but his eyes reminded her of winter.

'But you've patched things up?' she said, wondering what on earth they could have argued about to cause such a terrible rift. She only saw her own parents and sister every month or so, but she couldn't imagine not seeing them at all.

'Yes. At the ripe old age of thirty-eight, I decided that pride was a poor substitute for family.'

'You mean whatever happened was your fault?'

'It certainly wasn't anyone else's.'

He sounded so grim and private that Angela found herself flinching away. Then, when she shook off a sudden sense of danger and placed a tentative hand on his arm, she felt his muscles contract as if she'd touched him with a match.

'I'm glad you made the effort to make things right,' she said, refusing to be put off by his frown. 'I'm fond of your father.'

'So am I.' His fingers circled her wrist, and, when she gave an involuntary shiver of anticipation, very deliberately he pulled her forearm over the edge of the recliner and placed her palm on his thigh. 'I'd also like to put things right with you.'

Angela gasped, snatched her hand away, and wrapped both arms protectively round her waist.

To her fury, Ryan's frown turned into a taunting, maddeningly seductive smile. 'Scared of me?' he asked softly. 'Then I must have been mistaken after all. For a moment there I had an idea you were the kind of woman who likes to play with fire.'

'I'm the kind of woman who dislikes rude, tactless, arrogant men,' she informed him, in a voice that, infuriatingly, she couldn't hold quite steady. Dear lord, the feel of that hard thigh beneath her fingers . . .

To her continued consternation, he only laughed. 'Are you indeed? In that case there are one or two things you ought to understand about me.'

For a reason she couldn't explain, Angela stopped feeling indignant and felt frightened. 'No,' she said. 'There's nothing I need to understand about you. I must be going.' She started to rise from the hassock, but Ryan put his hand on her shoulder and held her down.

'You're not going anywhere,' he said conversationally, and with total assurance.

'But why — ?'

'Because you dropped your jacket in my path, and I've decided it's time you knew that I only play games with all my cards on the table.'

'What do you mean?' She shifted uncomfortably under the weight of his hand.

He shrugged. 'Chemistry. We both know it's there, and I'll admit that I meant to resist it. It seemed — wiser, and perhaps kinder. But we're both adults. As long as you know exactly where you stand — '

'I stand right here on my own two feet,' she cried, squirming out of his grasp and springing up. 'And you can go right on resisting. I don't want your cards, Ryan Koniski.'

'Don't you? You could be right.' He stretched corded arms above his head and the gaze that met hers was as calm and inscrutable as she had ever seen it. 'What are you afraid of, Angela?'

'I'm not afraid of anything.'

'Lucky girl. I'm afraid of a great many things.'

'Your problem,' she snapped, and then added less aggressively, because, incomprehensibly, he was smiling that slow, impossible smile again, 'I don't like spiders.'

The smile broadened. 'I promise you I'm not spinning a web. Is that what frightens you? The terrifying prospect of being caught?'

'Caught?'

'In the bonds of matrimony perhaps? If that's the case, you have nothing to fear from me. Or is it just that you enjoy the chase, then don't know what to do once the prey is caught?'

'Don't be ridiculous.' She tossed her head, and her soft hair flew around her face. But Ryan looked so delectable, and so unexpectedly warm and amused, that she found herself admitting, 'I don't bother much with the chase any more, so there's not the slightest danger of matrimony. I'm not interested.'

'Hmm. I'm told divorce often has that effect.'

'Presumably it does.' Angela wondered how she came to be kneeling on the hassock again.

Ryan said nothing further, but his

eyes were deep grey and hypnotic, and she discovered that for no reason that made any sense she wanted very much to tell him about that long-ago heartache. It wasn't that he even seemed to care, but there was something about the way he was looking at her that made her need him to understand what had happened.

'Kelvin and I weren't married long,' she said abruptly.

'No?'

His tone was not unsympathetic, so she hurried on. 'No. We met when we were both students. He was studying law too, but two years ahead of me. I was enormously smitten and much too anxious to please him — with the result that he took me for a sweet, biddable yes-woman — no, don't laugh — so of course once he graduated he expected I'd willingly quit college and move wherever his career took him.' She sighed. 'He didn't think *my* career was important, so as far as he was concerned it didn't matter where, or if,

I ever completed my degree.'

'But it did matter,' said Ryan. 'Couldn't you compromise?'

'Not as far as Kelvin was concerned.'

'So you divorced him.'

'No. I tried to work things out. But he wasn't interested — wanted total capitulation. I was young enough, and besotted enough then, to consider giving in to him — until the night when he came home and told me I wasn't the kind of wife he wanted — by which he meant a wife who would put all her energies into *his* career and forget her own.'

'And that convinced you to divorce him?'

She shook her head and stared at a small brown mark on the carpet. 'No. He brought a friend with him that evening. A pert little brunette called Cecilia. I think he'd already decided she'd make a much better dogsbody than I would. It was Kelvin who divorced *me* in the end.'

'Poor Angela. The woman scorned.'

She frowned, surprisingly hurt by his flippancy. 'Not a bit of it. The woman greatly relieved. I should never have married him.'

She hadn't been relieved at the time, though, she recalled wryly. She'd been devastated and desperately unhappy. It had taken her a long time to adjust to the failure of her marriage, and the probability that she would never raise the family she had hoped for. Two girls and a boy, she had thought . . .

Ryan was watching her as if he guessed what she was thinking, and she remembered that it wouldn't do to let this cool, walking sex-symbol sprawled beside her know every detail of her fluffy girlish dreams.

'So you came to an amiable parting of the ways, did you?' he said now, nodding sagely. 'I see.'

'More or less.'

Less really, she mused, watching the light from the window play across the strong bones of his face as he closed his eyes and leaned his head against the back of the recliner. She had been glad to put the divorce behind her, of course, but she had never liked being forced to admit defeat, and she had married Kelvin with so much love and hope. The end of hope had also meant the end of a naïve belief in happily-ever-after. After Kelvin, and because there was no sense looking for further grief, she had given up expecting ever-after.

Her left leg began to go to sleep, and she shifted restlessly on the hassock. It *would* have been nice to have children, she thought, her gaze on the dark lashes sweeping down Ryan's cheek. Even sticky children with jam-covered faces . . .

'Angela, you're out of your mind,' she muttered out loud.

When his eyes snapped open and fastened on her with sudden concentration, she realised her habit of talking to herself was beginning to get out of hand. It came of spending too much time by herself.

'I have to go,' she said, jumping up again.

'Do you?' He rose too, with a feline grace that made her swallow hard. 'Why the hurry? I haven't even given you a drink.'

'I don't want a drink.'

'Hmm.' He stood looking down at her, his tall frame unnaturally still, and he was so close now that she could feel heat coming from his body. 'I wonder what you do want, Angela?'

'Not you,' she said quickly, because the look in his eye was of the speculative, predatory kind. 'You didn't put your cards on the table, remember?'

'Only because you wouldn't let me. And I'm not sure it matters after all.'

'What do you mean?' She tried to move away, but her feet seemed glued to the oriental carpet.

'Just that I'm beginning to realise we may very well hold the same hand. I believe you're a lot more like I am than I thought.'

'What . . . ?' She stopped, struck

dumb by the message in his eyes, as very deliberately he closed the space between them and dragged her into his arms.

It didn't even occur to her to struggle. For a moment he just held her while he gazed down into her face. Then his full lips parted so that she caught a glimpse of even white teeth.

'What the hell,' he said softly — and covered her mouth with his own.

The floor beneath Angela's feet seemed to dissolve into a cresting tide of elemental sensation. For a while she was conscious of nothing beyond the touch of his hands on her back and the sensuous delight of a kiss that was like no other she had known. Relentlessly, expertly, his tongue tantalised her lips, teasing them apart until her only desire was to respond to him with every straining muscle in her body.

Without thinking, because she had lost the ability to think, Angela wrapped her arms around his neck.

For a long moment they clung

together, and she sensed in Ryan a hunger that equalled, or even surpassed, her own. Then with a quick motion he circled her hips with his hands and pulled her against him so that she was excruciatingly aware of every virile inch of him, from the solid bareness of his legs, past his hips and rapidly beating heart to the vein throbbing wildly in his neck. Her hands began to explore the breadth and hardness of his back until, very gradually, she became aware that he wasn't responding any more.

'What is it?' she asked, tilting her head to look up at him.

'Nothing that can't be resolved. If I'm not mistaken, the grapevine has let us down royally.'

'The grapevine?' Angela shook her head to clear it, and came down to earth with a thud. Had Ryan gone clean out of his mind?

'Mm. Listen,' he said.

Angela listened. A door slammed, and then she heard Charlotte Koniski say soothingly, 'Never mind, Harry, I'm sure there'll be more going on in town next week. It's just that everyone's getting ready for the weekend.'

'See what I mean?' Ryan murmured into her ear. 'Dad hasn't been able to turn up any gossip worthy of the name, so Aunt Charlotte has persuaded him to come home. Now she can tuck him up on the sofa and drive him crazy with thermometers, wet compresses and cold drinks.'

'Yes, but — hey!' Suddenly Angela became aware that Ryan's arms were still locked around her waist, and that his hands were carelessly caressing her rear. Any moment now her reputation for discretion, common sense and businesslike decorum would be in tatters. 'Ryan, they're coming in here . . . '

'Mm,' he agreed imperturbably. 'So they are. Hello, Dad, Rob, Aunt Charlotte. Have a good drive?'

4

Harry Koniski's bushy grey eyebrows beetled upwards. 'Harrumph,' he rumbled.

'Yes, dear, we had a very nice drive,' said Charlotte firmly. 'And we brought Rob home.'

'I thought I recognised him,' said Ryan, smiling at her. He dropped one arm from Angela's waist and turned her so that she stood pressed against his side. 'As you see, company called while you were out, but I hope I've managed to entertain her.'

As Angela's face turned a very unbusinesslike pink, Rob let out a shout of laughter, and Harry said, irritably, 'It's time you learned to behave yourself, my boy.'

Angela choked back a groan. For the life of her she couldn't decide if she wanted to kick Ryan for his unmitigated gall, or burst out laughing at the idea of anybody, even his father, calling this forceful, thirty-eight-year-old power-broker 'my boy'.

In the end she only murmured, 'Nice to see you on your feet again, Harry. I came to bring you some books.' There was really nothing else she could say that wouldn't land her even further in the glue.

'Harrumph,' said Harry again. 'Thank you.' He frowned, and the bushy eyebrows rose up to meet an equally bushy head of hair. 'Didn't realise you knew my son so well.'

'She didn't until Rob went to work for her,' said Ryan easily. Then he added in quite a different tone, 'But I suppose you might say she still doesn't.'

'Well I think it's very nice, dear,' said Charlotte. 'Angela, I can see my nephew hasn't made you any tea — '

A snort came from the direction of the doorway, where Rob stood loafing against the wall with a wide grin splitting his freckled face. '*Tea!*' he exclaimed. 'Huh. He was too busy making Ms Badd — '

But Rob never got to finish his sentence. In a voice that cracked with authority, Ryan snapped, 'That will do, thank you, Rob. Angela, I believe you were just on your way.'

'Now, Ryan,' Charlotte remonstrated, patting the tight brown bun coiled on the top of her head, 'be nice, and let Angela decide — '

'She's decided,' said Ryan. 'Haven't you, Angela? Come on, I'll see you to your car.'

She thought of telling him that she was quite capable of responding to his aunt's invitation without his input, and that she'd very much enjoy a cup of tea. But the truth was, she was as anxious to leave the Koniski home as he was for her to go. It was difficult to maintain even a semblance of her usual breezy composure when Rob was openly ribald, Harry suspicious, and Charlotte beaming the fond smile of a born matchmaker. As for Ryan — he was just impossible.

'Thank you,' she said to him coolly. 'I can see myself out. Harry, I'm so glad you're better. Charlotte, I'll take you up on the tea another time . . .'

'Once the coast is clear, you mean?' Ryan allowed his hand to slip down her hip as he ignored the rebuff and hustled her across the room and out of the door.

On the step she turned to look up at him. Dusk tinted the sky and cast deep purple shadows across his face. 'Did you *have* to make us into an exhibition?' she demanded. 'Now they all think — I mean, if you'd just let me go the moment you heard them come in — '

'And have them find us standing at opposite sides of the room like a couple of guilty kids caught playing doctor? Why should I?' He moved his hand from her hip and spread it across her lower back.

'Because it would have been the gentlemanly thing to do,' said Angela, who couldn't think of a more compelling reason to offer him — or one less likely to cut any ice.

'Whatever gave you the idea that I'm a gentleman?' he drawled — predictably, in Angela's opinion.

'My mistake.' She twisted away from him and stepped on to the gravelled pathway. 'I should have known better.'

'Yes, you should,' he agreed, as she hurried towards her new silver Buick. But when she wrenched open the door, suddenly overwhelmed by the need to escape, Ryan's hand descended lightly on her shoulder.

'Come to Seattle with me,' he said, and the words, softly spoken, were more of a command than a request.

Angela stared up at the sky. It was shot with flames of dark blue and orange as the sun sank below the horizon. The scent of Charlotte's azaleas hung heavy on the warm evening air.

Turning to face him, she said quietly, 'I can't do that.' A very faint breeze lifted the hair on her neck, and she added without thinking, 'When are you leaving? Rob said you'd be gone by today.'

'Rob doesn't always listen. I said I'd like to be gone by today. Hell, I'd like to have left a week ago.'

'So when *are* you leaving?'

'As soon as Dad's back on his feet. Maybe the end of the week.'

'Oh.' Angela stared at her hand. It was clasped so tightly over the wheel, it looked like wax.

'Why did you kiss me?' she asked suddenly.

'Because I wanted to. You wanted it too.'

'No,' said Angela. 'No, that's not . . . ' She stopped because what he said was true. She had wanted him to kiss her right from that moment, a few weeks ago, when she had stood at her office window and watched him move towards her across the street. 'Yes,' she admitted. 'You're right. I did. And now you have, so that's that.'

'Is it?'

'Of course.'

'I don't see why.' He eased his hand over her shoulder and began a gentle massage of her neck. 'Come with me when I leave, Angela. Mrs Rainbow will be away for the weekend, and my apartment has all the amenities.'

'I'm sure it has, but I have an office to run.'

'On a Saturday? You don't work weekends, do you?'

'Sometimes.'

'But not the next one,' he said, with irritating certainty.

'No. But why *should* I go away with you, Ryan? I mean — '

'I'd have thought it was obvious.' She felt his fingers catch in her hair and his grey eyes were dark with a meaning she couldn't possibly mistake.

'Just like that? Just, Come and jump into my bed? Is that what you're saying?'

'Well, what did *you* have in mind?' Now the eyes challenged her, forcing her to face up to the truth.

And the truth was that she had had

precisely that in mind almost from the moment they first met.

'Were those the cards you wanted to put on the table?' she asked dully, wondering why something that for a few ecstatic seconds had seemed vital and wonderful seemed to have degenerated into a game of poker.

'No. Those were different cards. The kind I'd deal to any woman who wanted more than I'm able to give her. But you don't, do you? We're two of a kind. Your needs are no more and no less than mine.' He spoke with a faint note of disparagement, as if he thought she ought to want more.

'I don't know. What *are* your needs?' She wished he would move his hand but, inexplicably, she didn't have the will to tell him so.

'I'm a man, Angela. You're a woman. A particularly intelligent one. I don't think you need me to draw a picture.'

No, she didn't need a picture. Ryan, who had originally looked on her as a reluctant divorcee on the prowl for a replacement for her mate, had discovered that she was as comfortable with the single state as he was. Which, from his point of view, threw a whole different light on the matter of a weekend's casual sex in Seattle. Handy to his place of work too, she thought cynically.

'No.' Her reply was sharp.

'No?' Ryan raised his eyebrows.

'No, I'm not interested in filling the current vacancy in your bed. You'll have to find some other willing tenant.'

He shrugged, and replied without visible resentment, 'I suppose I could if I chose to. But I'm particular about my tenants, Angela. I think you'd suit me very well.'

'Too bad. You wouldn't suit me.'

'You'll never know if you don't try me,' he said, with the sort of careless smile that told her it didn't matter to him much.

'That's my problem,' she snapped.

Ryan removed his hand from her neck and she scrambled awkwardly into her car. But as she fumbled in her bag for the keys, he rested an arm along the back of the seat and leaned inside. When she looked up, her mouth falling open in surprise, he bent his head and brushed a careless kiss across her forehead.

'Goodnight, Angela. Sweet dreams,' he murmured. Before she could gather her wits he had turned his back on her and was strolling away up the path.

Inside the house, someone turned on a light, and its beam fell across Ryan's head and shoulders so that for a moment he resembled some mythical hero rising up out of the darkness to inspire hopeful mortal maidens with a fearful joy. Except that she was a thirty-five-year-old lawyer, not a hopeful maiden, Angela reminded herself with a firm shake of her head.

The light was turned off again, and Ryan disappeared into the house.

Once inside, he didn't return to the family waiting expectantly in the living-room, but leaned heavily against the door and shut his eyes. Angela Baddingley. That woman was getting under his skin in ways he wouldn't have thought possible a week ago, when he'd been convinced she was just another lonely divorcee on the make. Even then he'd found her attractive, he acknowledged. But not fair game. Now that she'd flatly turned him down, though, it was a different matter. She wasn't the vulnerable creature he'd imagined — the one he had been determined not to hurt. She was a thoroughly modern 'ms' who was more than capable of looking out for herself.

He opened his eyes again and smiled into the shadows. And *he* was a thoroughly modern man who for years now had gone after what he wanted. And usually got it. Especially since Amy and, more importantly, Connie, had taught him not to look for commitment. A man like him was asking for trouble if he expected that — asking to get kicked royally in the teeth. He had known that for a long time now, he reflected, with a bitterness that surprised him by its force. Still, on the whole, his life suited him.

As outspoken, independent Angela would suit him — for a while.

Smiling thoughtfully, he strolled into the living-room to face the inevitable curiosity of his family.

★ ★ ★

'What's wrong, Ms Baddingley? You look like an over-watered cactus.' When Angela raised a jaundiced-looking eyebrow, Rob pushed his chair back from his desk and explained, 'You know. Sort of prickly and waterlogged. Rough weekend?'

Angela pinched in her mouth and tried very hard not to be amused. 'As a matter of fact I had a very quiet weekend,' she replied repressively, picking up a paperclip and uncurling it into a useless piece of wire.

Prickly and waterlogged indeed. Rob certainly had a way with words when he bothered to use them — but he was probably right.

She had spent the weekend ruthlessly uprooting weeds, cobwebs, dust and birdseed from even the remotest corners of her house and garden. Not a wall or an appliance remained unscrubbed. And all the time she had been working, at the back of her mind she had known she was figuratively scrubbing Ryan out of her life.

It hadn't worked, though, she thought glumly, because ever since he had kissed her she had been unable to stop thinking about him.

That kiss had been almost unbearably intoxicating, and Ryan was right that she had wanted it — right that she had wanted much more. But for a reason which she couldn't understand she had been furious with him for suggesting that her needs were as casual and hedonistic as he freely admitted his own were. Would she have been any less offended if he had continued to think of her as some lonely creature looking for a permanent partner? If that was the case, she must be going soft in the head. And she had no reason to resent him for being as direct and to the point about what he wanted as she was herself.

It was true that she didn't look for commitment. Had actively avoided it since her marriage, accepting the occasional date, but generally sublimating her natural instincts in her work. The one time she had allowed a relationship to go on for any length of time — with John, a widowed businessman from Port Angeles — the two of them had eventually come to the conclusion that the only thing they really had in common was a serious passion for chocolate ginger. Much less serious was a superficial physical attraction.

Angela made a face, then, seeing Rob's grin, hastily composed her features.

Perhaps she had known from the beginning that John was safe. Safe because there was no chance of lasting love.

But Ryan wasn't safe. Ryan was a drug she couldn't stop craving. Which was probably why she was prickly.

'Ryan's been acting like a cactus too,' she heard Rob mutter, as if he'd been reading her thoughts.

'Really?' replied Angela, pulling herself together and speaking in her best regally disinterested voice.

'Uh-huh. Mr Koniski — Mr Harry, I mean — told him he'd probably have another heart attack if Ryan didn't stop snapping like a turtle and staring at Aunt Charlotte's cooking as if he thought it might be going to bite him back. And Aunt Charlotte told him — '

'I know,' said Angela. 'Charlotte told him he ought to be nice. But he's not nice.'

'Huh.' Rob stood up and wandered over to the window. 'He is, you know. It's just that he doesn't really trust anyone but himself. And unless they're his clients, he doesn't much like people needing him.'

Angela glanced up sharply. She'd

never heard Rob speak at such length before, or in quite that tone — as if he was serious for once, and as if he knew something about Ryan that she didn't.

'What makes you say that?' she asked quietly.

Rob shrugged, and went on staring at the street.

'Rob?' Angela persisted. 'I asked you a question.'

'Yup, well, you know . . . '

'No, I don't.'

The young man swung round, hitched his hip on the sill, and assumed an unusual interest in his shoes. 'I guess maybe you wouldn't,' he muttered. 'But Ryan told me himself, so I thought you — I mean you and he seemed kind of — um . . . ' He cleared his throat.

'Friendly?' suggested Angela, with a warning note in her voice.

'Yup, friendly.' He looked up, beaming, as if she'd come up with the right answer to a riddle.

'And?' she prompted.

'And so I thought you knew.'

'Knew *what?*' Angela wondered if she'd miss his head and break the window if she threw her paperweight at him.

'That Ryan — I mean, you *do* know, don't you . . . ?' As Angela lifted the paperweight, he finished quickly, 'That Ryan once spent three years in prison.'

★　★　★

Shock. Disbelief. Denial. Angela reached for her coffee-cup, stared blankly at the unappetising sludge in the bottom, and put it down.

Much later, she was to wonder why Rob's bombshell had made her feel as if he'd tossed her into a tub of iced gin. But now, at this moment, it was all she could do to keep afloat. She felt cold all over, and there was a bitter, burning sensation in her throat.

'Ms Baddingley, are you all right?' Rob's anxious query finally penetrated the nether reaches of her brain, and she discovered she was carefully removing all the staples from her stapler, and flipping them out on to the floor.

'Yes, of course. I'm fine.' She put the stapler down, lifted her head, and gave him what she hoped was a nonchalant smile. 'I was just surprised, that's all. Are you sure Ryan actually told you that — that he'd been in gaol?'

'Yup. When he agreed to defend me. Said he'd been where I was himself, and he didn't want to see another young fool who ought to know better end up the way he had. He was shouting at me, because I'd told him I didn't need any damn lawyer.'

'Ryan? Shouting?' repeated Angela dazedly, not sure whether to believe him or not.

'Yup. Only time I've seen him lose his temper. Ms Baddingley, I didn't mean to say something I wasn't meant to — '

'Why not?' asked Angela, beginning to regain both her breath and her perspective. 'Everyone else does around here. Except when it comes to Ryan, and I suppose that's only because of

Harry.' She paused for a moment and then went doggedly on. 'Rob — now that you've started — what did Ryan actually *do?*'

Rob shook his head. 'Don't know. Didn't ask him. Wouldn't have told me.'

'I suppose not,' agreed Angela. 'He's not exactly forthcoming about his past.' She picked up a pen and tapped it on the edge of her desk.

Things were at last beginning to fall into place. The reticent, self-contained man, toughened by years behind bars, forced to look out for himself — it was only natural he would be careful with his affections, reluctant to allow anyone close. In fact it was surprising that he still knew how to laugh — occasionally even at himself.

Looking up, she saw that Rob was eyeing her as if he thought she might be about to assault the stapler again. She pushed her glasses firmly back up her nose. This wouldn't do. What Ryan had or hadn't done in the past was no business of hers — even if she was dying of curiosity, along with a reluctant sympathy for that difficult man which she was damned if she meant to acknowledge. If Ryan had been sent to prison, it must have been for good reason. And, knowing him, it wasn't likely he would thank her for any kind of misplaced sentimentality. Nor was it good for office morale for her to behave like a Victorian spinster who had just caught her first glimpse of a man's legs. Or, in this case, Ryan's feet of clay.

Young Rob was looking worried, and *she* was supposed to be the one in charge. Besides, old Mrs Gruber, having nothing better to do, would be in to change her will for the fifth time this year at any moment — and if Mrs Gruber caught even a whiff of a rumour that the local attorney's behaviour might be worth keeping an eye on it would be all over town in five minutes.

'Let's get back to work,' said Angela briskly. 'The Koniskis' affairs are no concern of ours.'

She managed to hold fast to this view

for the next several days as she busied herself with work and refused even to think about Rob's revelation. Presumably Ryan had gone back to Seattle, and that was that. She could ask Rob, of course, but she didn't intend to.

'A hunk that passed in the night,' she murmured wryly to Al, one evening at the end of the week.

'Grack,' agreed Al sympathetically.

'Yes, that's all very well,' Angela groaned. 'But why, *why* am I so obsessed with that man?'

Al pulled busily at a strand of her hair, and Angela gave up hoping he would inspire her.

'I don't know,' she muttered, sinking on to her well-made, fawn-coloured sofa and punching a dent in a chocolate-brown cushion. 'If I had any sense — which I've always thought I had — I'd put him right out of my mind.'

Al detached the hair from her scalp with a triumphant, 'Grack.'

Angela said, 'Ouch,' and jumped up,

rousing Al to a frenzy of squawking and flapping. After a moment's hesitation, she marched out into the garden.

It was dark now, quiet and peaceful with the waves washing gently against the cliff, and she allowed the scents and the sounds of the night to enfold her in their ageless magic.

After a while the phone rang, and she coaxed Al on to her finger and walked back into the house.

It was Sarah Jackson calling to remind her that she'd promised to attend the Caley Cove Annual Charity Ball on Saturday night. This year it was to be held in the ballroom of the Cove Resort Inn, a new and glamorous edifice built in the hope of attracting exclusive tourist business.

'I bought a ticket,' she told Sarah. 'But that doesn't mean I have to go, does it?'

'Yes it does,' said Sarah. 'Brett's escaped to a veterinary convention, Dad refuses to go, and if you don't come I'll have to sit with Mom and Mrs

Bracken and listen to them dissecting the other guests.'

Angela laughed. 'All right. If you put it like that . . . '

'I do,' said Sarah, and hung up.

Angela thought nostalgically of the days when she had told Sarah what to do.

All the same, she went at once to her bedroom to select a sleeveless white silk dress with red accessories.

★　★　★

The band was already tuning up by the time Angela and Sarah strolled into the glittering and crowded ballroom just after nine o'clock. But the lights had not yet been dimmed and it was very hot.

'Over there,' said Angela, guiding her visibly pregnant friend through the jostling throng to a reasonably secluded table in the corner. 'Whew!' She fanned her face with a napkin, settled Sarah in a chair and sank down thankfully into

the one beside her. 'Do you think . . . ?'
She stopped.

A man was standing in front of her. A tall man with tawny-gold hair who was obviously not in Seattle. He was holding out his hand.

'Good evening, Angela,' said Ryan. 'The first dance is mine, I believe.'

5

Angela stared at the outstretched hand. It was a large, capable-looking hand, with short blunt nails and a diagonal scar across the knuckles. She hadn't noticed that scar before. Only the one on his forehead. She raised her eyes with a feeling she'd be wiser to turn tail and run.

Ryan was smiling. An easy but implacable smile that turned her stomach to curdled cream and her legs to jelly.

'What are you doing here?' She managed to speak clearly, indicating only a mild interest. What she had to suppress was an unforgivable urge to blurt, Ryan, what did you *do*?

'I'm asking you to dance,' he said, as if he were explaining a very simple fact to a child.

'Yes, but . . . no. No, thank you. I'd rather not.'

'All right, I'll rephrase that. I was not *asking*.' He seized her wrist. 'Come along, Ms Baddingley; you and I are about to kick up our heels.'

'I never kick . . . ' began Angela.

'Then it's time you started.'

She heard Sarah smother a giggle as Ryan hauled her on to her feet, placed his arm around her waist as if it belonged there, and began to guide her briskly round the floor.

At first the only thing Angela felt like kicking was Ryan Koniski. Then gradually, as the pressure of his hard body began to warm her — silk on silk, she thought dizzily — and she felt the smoothness of his shirt stroke her cheek, she stopped wanting to do anything but kiss him.

There were other couples around them but she was hardly aware of their existence. The music slowed, and she put her hands on his shoulders and raised her lips.

'Waiting to be kissed?' he asked conversationally.

'Oh! How — ?'

'How dare I? I've risked more than a kiss in my time, Angela, darling. Sometimes to my cost.'

Angela returned to reality with an almost tangible thump. Yes, apparently he had. To his very considerable cost.

'For example?' she asked, curiosity temporarily overcoming lust.

'I'll tell you some day. When the time is right. At the moment I've more important things to do.'

'Such as?'

'Oh . . . ' his eyelids drooped suggestively ' . . . such as this.'

'What . . . ?' Her words were cut off as his mouth came down hard on hers and both his arms locked around her ribcage.

Vaguely, she was conscious of music, slow and erotic, and of heat, and people shuffling around them. Then where they were, what planet they were on, ceased to have any meaning, because the only reality was Ryan. He was part of her, she could feel him in every singing vein of her body, and who he was, and what he had done, didn't matter. Even as some small core of sanity deep inside her tried to tell her that this was the wrong place, the wrong man, and probably the wrong year, she moved her arms and clasped them around his neck.

It was, or seemed to be, a long time later when she became aware that the music had stopped. Chandeliers threw flickering pin-points of light against the walls, and there was a sudden, crackling stillness in the ballroom.

It lasted less than a second.

'Imagine! In full view of everyone . . . '

'Angela Baddingley, of all people . . . '

'That Ryan Koniski! Hasn't changed a bit. I'll bet he only came back to make trouble.'

As she came down to earth, Angela heard the silence fractured by murmurs of delighted disapproval. She remembered, too late, that she lived in a very small town.

The music started up again, and she

said to Ryan, 'Damn you,' as she tried to tear herself out of his arms.

'And where do you think you're going?' he asked, holding her firmly.

'Back to Sarah. Ryan, let go. Everyone's looking.'

'I know. And enjoying themselves immensely. It's beginning to feel quite like old times.'

'Ryan, I said let go.' She stopped struggling and spoke in a furious stage whisper, because a dozen pairs of eyes were still riveted their way, and a dozen necks seemed likely to get a permanent crick. When he didn't let go, but continued to guide her around the floor, she plastered a brilliant smile on her face, tilted her head back as though she were responding to some conversational gambit, and said softly, 'Ryan Koniski, if you don't let me go this minute, I'm going to scream.'

'Good,' said Ryan. 'It'll make a nice change from all that icy stand-offishness interspersed with bouts of steamy passion. And this scandal-loving cesspool will relish every moment.'

Angela gritted her teeth and tried again. 'But I won't. And I'd appreciate it if you'd stop using me as a pawn in some private vendetta against this town.'

'Is that what you think? I couldn't care less about Caley Cove, Angela. I stopped caring a long time ago.' He took her hand and trapped it against his chest, and when she looked at his face she saw that he was telling the truth. The town where he'd grown up could be wiped off the map for all he cared.

'Maybe you couldn't, but *I* happen to live here,' she said coldly.

'Then maybe you should have thought of that before you responded to my kiss with such gratifying gusto. You'd have had the whole ballroom on your side if you'd slapped my face. But don't worry. One kiss won't do your business any harm. Might even be good for it.' His grip on her hand tightened and he swung her expertly around a potted palm.

'Do you think so? Then you're a cynic as well as a bastard.' Angela continued to smile brilliantly. 'I suppose you think good business makes it all right for you to ride roughshod over everyone else?'

She watched his mouth turn down in a familiarly sexy curve. 'Not everyone. Just you. And only because you want me to — although you pretend you don't.'

'Hasn't anyone told you that that kind of male arrogance went out with — with the telex and long-playing records?'

Ryan stood stock-still, and when he let out a bark of surprisingly genuine laughter all the craning necks jerked straight upwards. 'At least you admit I'm only a few years out of date,' he replied, the laughter still in his eyes. 'Surely I can be forgiven for that. Besides, you did want me to kiss you.'

He spoke with such genuine amusement, even affection, that Angela found herself smiling sheepishly back.

It was true. She *had* wanted him to kiss her. In fact she wouldn't at all mind if he did it again. But not here, with most of Caley Cove looking on.

'You're impossible,' she sighed.

'Only impossible? I thought I was a bastard.'

'That too.' The lights dimmed, Ryan's leg pressed against her thigh, and she said desperately, 'Ryan, *please* take me back to Sarah. She's by herself . . . '

'That's better. I like it when you say please.' He gave her an approving little pat on the head.

Angela contemplated standing on his elegant black feet, but decided against it when he began to steer her back to the quiet corner of the ballroom where her friend sat waiting and alone.

Except that Sarah wasn't alone.

Harry Koniski and his sister, Charlotte, were seated on either side of her. All three of them were beaming the fond smiles of parents whose capricious offspring had finally settled down to responsibility.

Oh, my God, thought Angela. They think Ryan's serious about me. And they're pleased. Probably they set this whole thing up. Not that she could seriously imagine anyone setting Ryan up unless — unless they had his express co-operation . . .

'Evening, Angela.' Harry nodded at her. 'See my boy's monopolised you again.'

'No, really . . . ' began Angela, stepping sideways to put as wide a berth as possible between herself and the cause of her embarrassment.

Harry shook his head. 'It's all right. Didn't mean to snap your head off the other day.'

'Oh, you didn't . . . '

'No, he was snapping mine off, weren't you, Dad?' Ryan smiled at his father, and Angela saw fondness and a certain sadness in his eyes. 'It's a habit he got into long ago — when he expected the worst and usually got it.'

'Harrumph. That's all over now.'

'Of course it is,' Charlotte put in

quickly. 'Angela, dear, you do look nice. How are you?'

'I'm fine. But I can't stay long . . . '

'Of course you can,' said Sarah, looking her directly in the eye. 'What's the hurry?'

'Oh, well, if you want me to stay with you — '

'I don't. Go and enjoy yourself.'

'But you said — '

Sarah smiled a sphinx-like smile. 'I know I did. Taste of your own medicine, Angela. Remember when you insisted I go out with John Marlowe right after I broke up with Brett — because you said my long face was upsetting your clients?'

Reluctantly, Angela smiled back. 'Yes, but that was different. I haven't broken up with anybody.'

'That's because you haven't given anyone a chance to be breakable up with for ages.' Sarah grinned, and glanced over at Ryan. 'Until recently.'

Help! thought Angela. This whole thing has to be a put-up job. Most likely

Charlotte Koniski talked to Sarah's mother, who talked to Sarah . . . But how had they persuaded Ryan to fall in with their plans? She stole a glance at him. He was standing with his legs apart and his arms folded on his chest as he listened to the conversation with narrowed eyes. As if he found the subject of Angela's love-life truly absorbing. It couldn't be that he'd wanted to come to the ball — could it? It was just possible . . . No. She must head that thought off at the pass and get out of here as fast as she could. No point in letting things go further.

'Well, if you don't need me, Sarah — ' she began, tucking her sequinned bag beneath her arm.

'She doesn't. But I do.' Ryan took her hand, and pulled her back on to the dance-floor before she had the wit to resist him.

Once again that enervating languor began to sap the strength from her muscles. She knew that, if Ryan continued to hold her with the kind of easy possessiveness that made her feel as if he had the right, sooner or later she would end up delighting the entire ballroom by making a complete fool of herself. And not because she'd slapped his handsome face. Rather the opposite.

'I'd like a drink, please,' she murmured.

'Of course.'

He led her into an adjoining room where red leather chairs were grouped intimately around black lacquered tables, and for a few moments, while Ryan collected drinks from the bar, she was blessedly, thankfully alone.

Angela, she told herself sternly as she tried not to stare longingly at Ryan's formidable back, this is ridiculous. Either you give in, give him what he obviously wants, and then wait for him to exit from your life, or you get out of here right this minute before you're tempted to start behaving like an adulating groupie.

But Ryan was already on his way back with the drinks.

'I'm sorry, I've changed my mind,' she said quickly, before he had a chance to sit down. 'I'm feeling a little queasy — it's the heat, I expect — and I really think I'd better go home.'

'Chicken,' he taunted softly, setting the glasses on the table.

'I'm not — '

'Yes, you are.' He lowered himself into a chair. 'But suit yourself. Personally I intend to finish my drink. After which, if you insist, I'll take you home.'

'Not after drinking, you won't,' said Angela. She watched smugly as he took a long swallow of his gin. 'I'll take a taxi.'

He shrugged and fixed her with a bland grey gaze as he proceeded to empty the remainder of his glass.

Angela's eyes widened, and without even realising she was doing it she took a sip of her own gin and tonic. Ryan continued to watch her with that disconcerting stare.

'You shouldn't drink so fast,' she told him, when the stare and his cool silence began to raise goose-bumps on her arms.

'Shouldn't I? Ready to go?'

'Not with you.'

'Certainly with me. I'm sure Sarah's not ready to leave yet, and I've no intention of letting you take a taxi.'

'But you've been drinking.' She had him there, and she couldn't quite keep the note of triumph from her voice.

'Mm. One glass — '

'That's still too much.'

'Of soda water.'

'Oh.' She glared at him, because now *he* was the one looking smug.

'Well?'

'Well what?'

'What's your next pretext for refusing to let me drive you home? Surely you haven't run out of excuses already? Or have you decided to stay and dance with me some more?'

Out of the frying-pan into the fire, thought Angela grimly. Of course she could decide to stay and *not* dance with him, but somehow she had a feeling that might prove easier said than done. She hadn't been too successful about not dancing with him so far. And although she could just about put up with the whispers of the crowd there was no way she could stand the looks of hopeful approval on the faces of Aunt Charlotte and Harry.

As for Sarah — she would talk to her later.

'No,' she said slowly. 'I don't want to stay, but — '

'But you don't want me either. Angela, I offered you a lift, not a roll in the hay.'

Angela put down her glass with a clatter. 'That's a relief. Because I don't do hay,' she informed him.

Ryan suppressed a smile and tilted his head pensively to the side. 'No? No, I must say it doesn't seem your style. Silk sheets, then. Black ones, I think. And a sinfully soft feather bed. How would that suit you?'

Angela felt the blood rushing to her head. She also felt a familiar craving to commit violence on the person of Ryan Koniski. When the bartender's eyes flicked curiously in her direction, she suspected her fury showed on her face.

'What would suit me,' she said, rising to her feet with her best attempt at dignified restraint, 'would be to go home and get away from you. Goodnight, Ryan, and thank you for the drink.'

As she walked away from him without looking back, she tried not to think about his eyes. They hadn't shown the least sign of contrition. And just before she'd turned away from him she had made the mistake of looking over her shoulder.

He'd been laughing at her. Which was particularly maddening because up until tonight she had been convinced that laughter was a commodity he rationed. It was annoying to be proved so totally wrong.

She made her way across the ballroom, where the beat of the music throbbed up through the floor and only the younger couples remained gyrating blissfully beneath the rainbow-tinted lights.

'Sarah, I'm off,' she said to her friend, who was deep in baby-talk with Charlotte. 'You stay, of course. I'll get a taxi.'

'Oh. All right.' Sarah smiled brightly, and it was only afterwards that it occurred to Angela to wonder if the smile hadn't been altogether too complaisant. It was also much later when she remembered that it was unlike Sarah to leave a friend in the lurch.

She crossed the lobby without stopping to phone for a cab. On an occasion like this, there was probably one waiting outside.

There wasn't. Instead, a low-slung white Alfa-Romeo pulled up at the bottom of the steps just as she walked through the revolving doors. Without pausing to think, she carried right on revolving.

When she emerged into the air a second time, Ryan was waiting to grab her.

'Hey! I said I'm taking a taxi . . . '

'Fine. I'll play taxi, then, if that's what you want.'

'What I want is to be left alone.'

'Why? I assure you, Angela, that unless you choose otherwise all I plan to do is drive you home.' He paused on the bottom step and swung her around to face him. His eyes in the bright glare of the hotel lighting were smoky with exasperation. 'What the hell have I *done*?'

Angela opened her mouth, then closed it again so quickly that she bit into her tongue. He had asked her precisely the question she'd been dying to ask him all evening. What *had* he done? But this was not the time or the place to discuss the sins of his past. Nor, she supposed when she stopped to think rationally about it, was there any reason to refuse to get into his car. Whatever he had once been guilty of, she doubted if it had been assault on someone weaker than himself. Ryan was as overbearing as any man she had ever known, but deep in her gut she knew he wouldn't hurt her. Not physically anyway.

Deep in her gut, she also knew that it was another kind of hurt she was afraid of. Which was strange, because in all the years since Kelvin her heart had never once felt threatened by any man.

Kelvin . . . Funny, lately she'd been remembering the good times, when they were first married and so confidently in love. When they'd laughed together, and she hadn't yet taken in that Kelvin was only interested in his own needs — to the exclusion of hers. She sighed quietly. Twelve years was a long time to live without the love of a man . . .

No! Surely that wasn't what was happening to her now? She wasn't falling in love with Ryan? She squared her shoulders. No, of course she wasn't. And obviously there was no sense in refusing to let him give her a lift. She must be suffering from the effects of a summer heatwave that had gone on for a few weeks too long.

'You haven't done anything,' she said, answering Ryan's question coolly as he gripped her arms. 'At least nothing I know about. All right, then, you can take me home if you insist.'

He gave her a mocking little bow, and pretended to touch a non-existent cap. 'Thank you, madam. Very obliging of you, I'm sure.'

Angela didn't respond to what she had to admit was justifiable sarcasm. But when he opened the back door and bowed again, she was forced to explain, 'Oh, for heaven's sake, Ryan, don't be a jerk! I'm sitting in the front next to you.'

'Very condescending of you, madam.' His face was poker-straight as he pulled open the passenger door and waited stiffly while she thumped herself on to the seat. Then he swung himself in beside her and drove her home.

There was very little traffic, and the drive only took a few minutes. Minutes which, from Angela's point of view, were taut with tension. Ryan didn't speak, didn't look at her, and appeared totally oblivious to her presence. When he pulled into her driveway and stopped, she immediately flung open the door.

'Thank you. It was kind of you . . . '

But he was already standing on her side of the car.

When she climbed out and stared up at him in the silver light from the moon, she saw that his eyes shone silver too. 'I — it's all right. You don't have to see me to the house,' she mumbled, scrabbling in her bag for her key.

'I wasn't planning to.' He pushed his hands into his pockets and propped himself up against the car.

Angela turned her back and hurried away up the path. To her relief, the key turned in the lock without any embarrassing fumblings. Leave well alone, she told herself as she swung the door wide. Don't look back.

But of course she did look back, and Ryan was still standing there. His features were indistinct, but somehow she knew he was smiling that infuriatingly self-assured smile. And his hard, perfectly proportioned body stood out darkly, like an invitation to passion in the night.

He raised his hand in a careless gesture, but he didn't get back into the car.

Angela swallowed, clutched the door-jamb for support, and said in a voice that didn't sound as if it had much connection with her lungs, 'Would you like to come in?'

'Of course. What did you think I was waiting for?' He detached himself from the Alfa-Romeo and loped up the path with the swinging, easy stride of a natural athlete. Which, as far as Angela knew, he wasn't. But then what *did* she know about Ryan?

Belatedly, she realised what she'd done. But when she tried to change her mind and close the door on him, he put out one confident hand and held it open.

'Oh, no, you don't,' he said calmly. 'You asked me in, Angela. You can't chicken out on me now.'

'I certainly can if I . . . ' She stopped. That was the second time tonight he'd called her chicken. And a coward was one thing she wasn't. If she had to prove it to him, then so be it.

'I had no intention of taking back my invitation,' she lied airily, stepping aside as he strode into the hall. 'Would you like some coffee?'

'If it's expected of me.'

'What's that supposed to mean?'

He rested his hand on the wall above her head. 'If I told you I didn't want coffee, would you immediately assume I wanted something else?'

In his pitch-black suit, he seemed very large and a little menacing in the dimly lit hallway. Smooth, powerful and exuding a subtle aura of danger.

'Probably,' she admitted bravely. '*Don't* you?'

He ran his eyes briefly over the curves she knew were oh, so discreetly enhanced by the clinging white silk of her dress. 'Of course. What man wouldn't? But I don't aim to take it without your whole-hearted approval.'

'Which you won't get,' said Angela, wishing he'd drop his arm and move away.

As if he'd sensed her thoughts, Ryan straightened slowly. 'In that case, coffee it is,' he said, shrugging as he turned towards the living-room. 'Black with sugar for me.'

He didn't offer to help her, for which she was thankful. She desperately needed a few minutes to herself.

What on earth had she let herself in for, allowing this lethal man into her house? This ex-gaolbird with the body of a god, the persistence of a pneumatic drill, and a mind that was as closed to her as his past was. What would happen when she brought him the coffee he didn't want? She hit her forehead with the heel of her hand. What did she *want* to happen?

Abruptly Angela turned on the tap

and began to busy herself organising coffee, cups, a bowl of sugar and a jug of milk. On second thoughts, she mustn't think about what she wanted. Because she knew with an instinct that rarely let her down that getting what she wanted now would bring her grief. A grief perhaps greater than she had known when Kelvin left. That aching emptiness and disbelieving shock had healed much faster than she'd expected. But she was older now, and wounds didn't heal as quickly as the years passed by.

If she gave her heart to Ryan . . .

Good grief, what was she thinking of? She wasn't giving her heart to a man she knew nothing about. She was older all right, and that had better mean she was wiser.

Picking up a small metal tray, she slammed it down on the counter, loaded it with coffee and cups, and stamped out to join Ryan with a scowl on her face that should have made him run for his life.

In fact it only made him put down the bird book he was looking at, tilt his head against the back of her sofa and exclaim, 'Help! I do believe I'm about to die young. What's it to be? Poison? An axe? Or did you plan to strangle me with your bare hands?'

Angela put the tray down quickly. 'Accidental death, I think,' she replied, taken aback to find she wanted to giggle. It was amazing how quickly Ryan could change her mood.

'And dismemberment?' He sighed. 'I was afraid of that.'

'You're hopeless.' Angela gave up the attempt not to laugh.

'As well as a bastard and a jerk and impossible? Yes, I can quite see why you want to do me in.' He patted the seat beside him. 'OK, let's get it over with.'

All her doubts evaporated as if they had never existed, washed away by the potent power of Ryan's laughter, and the unyielding masculinity of the man she . . .

130

Oh, no. No! *Not* loved. She *couldn't* love Ryan.

She stared at him, aghast, and he smiled up at her with lips that were seductive, inflexible and irresistible.

Slowly, not wanting to, but unable to stop herself, she sank down on to the cushions beside him.

'Well?' He put his knuckles beneath her chin and made her look at him. 'Still want to do it? I see an effective-looking poker over there.'

Angela shook her head mutely. She wasn't angry any more — if she ever had been — just mesmerised by the compelling pewter-grey of his eyes.

'Good. In that case do you have an alternate programme in mind?' He smiled and rubbed a thumb across her cheek.

'No. But you have, haven't you?' The smooth, silken touch was an aphrodisiac, but his words restored a semblance of sanity.

'Not necessarily.' He removed his hand and stretched an arm along the back of the sofa. 'Not until you admit you want the same thing I do. For the same reasons.'

'What reasons?' asked Angela, knowing she didn't want to hear the answer.

'Pleasure. A moment of passion and closeness stolen from the solitude of life. I believe it's usually called sex.'

She gazed up at the firm line of his jaw, at the sardonic curve of his mouth, and the eyes that glinted with a light that was suddenly so bleak that her indignant response died on her lips.

'I believe it is,' she said quietly. 'Although I understand some lucky couples have another word for it.'

The corner of his lip curled in derision. 'Love? Is that your word? You're too old to believe in childish fantasies, Angela. But I'm sure you know that.'

'Yes,' she said, staring at the small pulse beating in his throat. 'I came to that conclusion myself. Years ago.'

She had too. Love *was* a fantasy. So why did she feel this strange tenderness for a man who was abrasive, dictatorial and apparently immune to the tender emotions? It wasn't just a physical attraction, although that was certainly there too in spades.

Ryan leaned forward and put both hands on her shoulders. 'Why are we playing these idiotic games?' he asked softly. 'I want you, Angela. And sooner or later I mean to have you.'

She gave a high, overly affected laugh as heat prickled all the way down her spine. 'Always the chauvinist,' she taunted. 'Has it never occurred to you that I might not mean to have you?'

He slid both his hands down her back so that their chests were almost, but not quite, touching. 'No. I'm not a chauvinist, though. That sort of arrogance was knocked out of me a long time ago. What I do know is that when a woman drops her jacket at my feet and uses her hazel eyes to lure me on she's after something. Sometimes it's money, sometimes marriage — maybe nothing more than a job. But with you I think it's none of those things. Which leaves — '

'Sex,' croaked Angela as one of Ryan's hands slipped below her waist.

'Mm. Shall we? In case you've forgotten, it's not nearly as bad as you make it sound.'

'I hadn't forgotten. I didn't . . . ' She stopped, started again, forcing herself to ignore the pressure of his palm across her rear. 'You're right. I do want you.' The admission came out in a whisper. 'But I can't — *won't* — go to bed with a man I know nothing about. As you said, I'm not a child any more. I do have some remnants of common sense. At least I hope I do.'

A mask seemed to slide over his face, shutting her out completely, and he stood up so abruptly that she gasped.

'What do you want to know?' He snapped the question out as if it were a bullet and she the unwilling target. As she sat gaping at him, he turned his back and stalked across to the window. The curtains hadn't been drawn, and his head was silhouetted starkly against the night.

Angela took a deep breath. It was now or never. And she had to know. It wasn't just idle curiosity. There were certain crimes that put a man beyond the pale — that would make him out of bounds to her forever.

She clenched her fists and pressed them into the cushion so that her arms were stiff as steel beside her hips. 'Rob told me,' she said, taking care not to raise her voice, 'that you once spent three years in prison. I'll understand if you'd prefer not to tell me, but — '

'But you're not about to bed the sort of man who had to be protected from other prisoners. That's what you're saying, isn't it? My God, Angela! You too. Do you honestly think — ?' He broke off abruptly. She could only see the outline of his face in the glass, but his disgust showed in the rigid way he was standing — head up, shoulders thrust back, and fists clenched hard on the sill.

He had read her mind so accurately that for a moment she was bereft of coherent speech. But when he didn't move, only stood there like some huge, menacing lion whose tail she'd twitched, she finally managed to say steadily, 'No. Not really. I don't know what to think. But — I'm sorry, I need to know what you did before I — '

'Before you honour me with your presence in my bed?'

His bitterness was so palpable, his tone so deliberately cutting, that Angela felt her own temper rising. She damped it down.

'It's my bed actually. And if you want to put it that way — yes.'

He swung round, ramming his hands into his pockets as if he needed to restrain them by force. From what she didn't even want to consider.

His eyes were the colour of wet slate. 'OK. You want to know. I'll tell you. I killed a man. The newspaper headlines called it murder.'

6

Slowly, very slowly, Angela's body lost its stiffness, and she sank back into the solid fawn upholstery of the sofa. She took in the hard angularity of Ryan's jaw, which seemed to be locked in combat with his face, and the bold, half-angry challenge in his eyes. She heard the flutter of insect wings against a window somewhere, and the faint, persistent hum from her fridge. And the seconds passed and she couldn't find her voice. Then, at last, she looked into Ryan's eyes again and saw beneath the defiance to the pain.

In that moment the horror of his revelation subsided, and for an instant she wanted to run to him and enfold him very gently in her arms.

But she knew she mustn't. For her own sake as well as for his.

'Why?' she asked at last. 'Can you tell me why?'

'After twenty years?' He laughed harshly. 'No, not really. It seemed the thing to do at the time.'

'The thing to do'. Had he actually said that? Was he calmly reducing murder to a whim? She narrowed her eyes to study him more closely. No. No, of course he wasn't. What he was doing was soldering up the chinks in his armour, trying to hide his feelings from the world. As he always did. Probably even from himself.

Especially, he was hiding them from her, with a fierce defensiveness.

Angela sighed. There was no point in pushing him, and she sensed that whatever had happened in his past had left Ryan with scars far deeper than the ones on his skin. Scars that the temporary satisfaction of a physical need could never heal. 'It's all right,' she assured him. 'You don't have to tell me.'

He shrugged and fixed his gaze on

the empty black cave of the fireplace. 'I know. Not that you'd have much trouble finding out. If you wanted to.'

'Why's that?' she asked quietly.

He turned his head, flicked her an ambiguous glance, then looked away again. 'Gossip. What else? The communication device most favoured in Caley Cove.'

'Oh.' Angela frowned, recognising that he'd withdrawn from her almost as if he had actually left the room. 'Ryan, gossip *isn't* favoured when it comes to you. Not really. Probably because people respect and like your father too much.'

'Respect and like? Feel sorry for, you mean.' He wheeled around and stalked across to the fireplace. She watched as he picked up the poker and began to weigh it absently in his hand.

'Perhaps,' she agreed, eyeing his weapon warily.

He flung it down abruptly, so that it clattered on to the hearth. 'OK,' he said, leaning against a corner of the mantel, and managing to sound as if he were discussing what not to have for breakfast. 'You want the gory details? You're not getting them. Suffice it to say I was eighteen and stupid, a source of constant worry to my father — which was precisely my intention in those days — and I got involved with an unsavoury crowd. I was known to the police, and when a body turned up outside a Seattle pool hall, and I turned up beside the body with a knife, it wasn't hard for them to put two and two together.'

Something was missing, Angela thought dazedly. A lot was missing. For one thing, in her heart of hearts, she couldn't believe Ryan was a killer.

'And were the police right?' she asked, smoothing her dress over her knees. '*Did* you kill him?'

'I suppose so. The verdict was guilty. Of manslaughter.'

'Then you didn't mean to kill him.'

'My dear Angela, I no longer know what I meant. There wasn't a lot of time to weigh options. Until later. I had three years to think about it then. And I don't propose to spend any more of my life trying to second-guess what's over and done with. Now — can we change the subject, or would you prefer me to leave?' He propped a highly polished shoe on the fender and raised his eyebrows as if he'd just told her he had once stolen an apple.

But he hadn't stolen an apple. He'd killed a man.

Angela tried to look away, but found she couldn't. She was mesmerised by his eyes. Vaguely, she was conscious that his mouth was flat and hard, like his body, and she knew that even as he tried to convince her that the past was over he didn't really believe it himself. The past was not over. It never would be for him. She knew also that if she told him to go he would leave her. Perhaps forever.

Whatever he'd done, she couldn't drive him away. Not now. Not after her questions had ripped open a deep and ancient wound.

'Yes, of course we can change the subject,' she said, trying to smile and not entirely succeeding. 'Tell me, what made you decide to take up law? And . . . ' She stopped. That was hardly changing the subject. It wasn't easy for a convicted felon to be admitted to the Washington State Bar.

Ryan's mouth twisted. 'What's the matter? Can't accept that an ex-gaolbird can turn into a respectable — and, I might add, *respected* member of the Bar?' He threw his head back, as if daring her to challenge his success.

Angela touched the garnets at her neck. 'I — no, it's not that, but — well, it must have been difficult. I mean . . . ' She allowed her voice to trail off, because she could think of no tactful way to ask this bitter, cynical man how in the world he had managed to convince the Bar Association that a knife-wielding punk could, as he had put it, turn into a respected attorney.

'Yes,' snapped Ryan, correctly interpreting her hesitation. 'It was difficult.

But as cases like mine are considered individually, I was able to convince the people who mattered that I could become an asset to the profession — and that my conviction was a miscarriage of justice. Does that satisfy your sense of propriety?'

Angela hung on to her temper by a thread. 'Was it a miscarriage of justice?' she asked, ignoring the taunting curve of his mouth.

He shrugged. 'Technically, yes. So I suppose you think that makes everything all right?'

'No,' said Angela, drawing a very deep breath. 'It most certainly doesn't make everything right. Contrary to a popular prejudice which even you seem to subscribe to, some lawyers are dedicated to the pursuit of justice. Not *injustice*. I happen to be one of them.'

She had the dubious satisfaction of seeing his eyes drop briefly, and when he looked up there was a warped sort of smile on his lips.

'*Touché*, Ms Baddingley. I believe I

deserved that. But don't worry about it too much. I wasn't exactly a misunderstood cherub.'

'But innocent of — deliberately killing a man.'

'Deliberately? No, it wasn't deliberate. Given the way I lived, perhaps inevitable. But not deliberate. The body on the ground could just as easily have been mine.'

Angela closed her eyes. She couldn't bear the image of Ryan lying motionless on some dirty pavement as all the vibrant life of him seeped away. Then, sensing that he would tell her no more than he already had, she returned to the subject of his chosen profession.

'They must have checked the transcripts of your trial.' she said slowly, 'or had some kind of evidence in your favour. Ryan, if you were innocent, why didn't you try to clear your name?'

'What for? There are degrees of innocence, and anyway the damage was done.' Abruptly he turned his back on her and, resting an elbow on the mantel, dropped his forehead on to his fist. When he spoke again his voice was uneven. 'I'd already lost three years out of my life, Angela. I couldn't get them back, and I'd no desire to waste any of the years I had left fighting the system. At least not as a plaintiff. I had a life to get on with, and besides, the people who mattered decided I was telling the truth. Finally.' The last word was ejected like an oath.

'But — you could have got compensation, some kind of payment . . . '

'And seen my name plastered all over the papers again? Further entertainment for the Caley Cove grapevine — Did you hear about that Ryan Koniski, my dear? He was on the news this morning, trying to make people think he didn't do it — of course we all know better, don't we? Poor, dear Harry . . . ' He swung round again and slammed his fist down on the mantel. 'Give me one good reason why I would want to put myself, or even the father I hadn't spoken to in three years, through that sort of punishment. I could have won, but I'm afraid gaol couldn't succeed in destroying my self-respect. I didn't need money, Angela. While I was locked up I came of age, and into a trust fund left me by my mother. By then all I cared about was getting on with what I wanted to do.'

'Yes. Yes, I think I understand.' Angela fixed her gaze on the tough line of his jaw because the pain and the pride in his eyes made her want to run to him and kiss away his hurt. She could imagine his reaction if she tried it. 'You wanted to help other people, didn't you?' she said with a sudden burst of intuition. 'People like Rob.'

'Did I?' Ryan's eyes flickered, then he closed his hand into a ball, turned it over, and appeared to develop a sudden interest in his nails. 'So you think I was motivated by some misguided desire to keep the Robs of this world from making the same mistakes I did. How altruistic of me.'

'Not misguided,' said Angela, accepting that Ryan found it hard to admit to caring about anyone, let alone his successors in the dock. She could see where prison might do that to a man. 'It's admirable and — '

'Ridiculously quixotic. Angela, I had more than one reason for going into law. For one thing, it passes the time. So do one or two other diversions.' He moved suddenly and came to stand in front of her. 'Well? Now that you've heard the story of my misspent and murderous youth, do you feel you know enough about me?'

Angela swallowed. She had by no means heard the whole story, there had to be a lot he wasn't telling her, but she knew better than to ask, Enough for what?

'No,' she said quietly. 'And I don't believe I ever will.'

'I see.' Ryan's tone was biting. 'So Caley Cove's righteous and upstanding attorney isn't about to be caught fraternizing with the criminal classes.

Very sensible. After all, you never know when I might decide to dispose of you, do you?'

Angela, who felt as if her emotions had been thrown into a blender and whipped, shredded and puréed for his benefit, found herself reeling from this harsh judgement of her character. 'No,' she said. 'That's not it at all. Ryan, I still don't know why you did what you did, or even *if* you did it — '

'Thank you for that much.'

She took a deep breath and stared fixedly at a black button on his suit. 'Please don't be sarcastic. The point is, I don't go in for one-night stands — '

'Fine. We'll make it a weekend.'

He was deliberately trying to provoke her. She was sure of it. But why? He said he wanted her. He knew she wanted him. But then, perhaps baiting her was his way of hiding his true feelings. Oh, if only he would just take her in his arms . . .

She pressed her palms together and clasped them tightly in between her knees. Did she really want him to make love to her? And if she did, why didn't she tell him so? Why didn't she stand up, take him by the hand and lead him into her bedroom?

No! She couldn't do that. Couldn't even think it. Because if she gave him the chance she knew beyond any doubt that he had it in his power to destroy her comfortably ordered existence without ever knowing he was doing it. And in the process he might also destroy her. She wasn't sure how she knew that, but she did.

After a while she raised her head, forced herself to meet the challenge in his eyes.

'I can't sleep with you,' she said in a voice that wasn't quite steady.

'Sleeping wasn't what I had in mind. Neither did you.'

He spoke lightly, as if the subject were something of a joke, but the chill that had been forming over her heart seemed to creep inside her veins like frozen mist.

Angela shivered. 'I know,' she said, stumbling to her feet and starting to edge her way around him. 'But I can't do — what you have in mind. I — I don't want to — '

'Liar.'

The softly murmured word hit her like a blow in the face, and without thinking she put a hand up to her cheek. 'No.' She shook her head violently. 'You don't understand. How could you, when I don't understand myself?' She pushed past him then, blindly, not knowing where she was going or what she intended to do. But long before she reached the door Ryan had caught her arm and pulled her back into the room.

'Hey,' he said. 'This is *your* house, remember. You can't run away on me, Angel.'

'I'm not . . . ' She stopped. His voice was much gentler than it had been, almost teasing. And she *was* running. From Ryan, who was, of necessity, a man who had learned to go after what he wanted. As he had made no secret of the fact that he wanted her.

'OK,' she said, taking a deep breath and looking him directly in the eye. 'I won't run. But how else can I convince you that I don't do casual sex?'

'You can start by pouring me a cup of that coffee — '

She blinked. Was he serious? And why the shift from cool, ungiving restraint to something like light-hearted banter? 'It's probably cold,' she said shakily.

He shrugged. 'I've survived a lot worse than cold coffee in my lifetime. So why not do as you're told? Then sit down beside me on that very practical sofa and tell me precisely what all this shrinking violet stuff is all about.'

Angela gave up and did as he said. She liked this determined but amiable man much better than the harsh-tongued ex-con, and as she poured the coffee, which was merely tepid, it crossed her mind that it was a very long time since any man had told her what to do and made her do it. Not that Ryan had made her exactly, but he was the sort of man who seemed to get his own way without making much of an effort.

Strangely, she was beginning to find she liked his way of ignoring the obstacles she put in his path, because, at least for the moment, she was absolved of the necessity to think.

'Now,' said Ryan, draining his cup in one gulp, 'you and I have a few matters to set straight.'

'Do we?' Angela fidgeted with her necklace, blood-red in the light from a table lamp, and wished she didn't feel a terrible urge to push her fingers through his tawnygold hair ... then across his back, and down further — much further.

'Mm.' His hands were closing over her upper arms and he was turning her so that their knees were very nearly touching. 'Sometimes, Angela, darling, you're so damn contrary I want to shake you. Unfortunately, I also happen to want you, a sentiment which you've told me you return. So — '

'So why am I being difficult instead of swooning obligingly into your arms?'

His lips tipped up in a sexy curve that belied their earlier hardness. 'Something like that.'

'In other words, you're saying it's time I got down to the business of solving your hormonal problems. Is that it?'

'No.' Ryan shook his head. 'For one thing, I doubt if it would do me any good to demand that sort of service — '

'You've got that right.'

He sighed. 'Angel, will you shut up and listen for two seconds? What I *am* doing is asking you why an attractive, intelligent woman with a normal libido — which I know you have — is behaving like a skittish virgin. Obviously *I've* learned to live with my past, but if you can't accept it — and believe me, it won't be the first time — '

'It's not that,' said Angela quickly. It wasn't either, even though he hadn't told her the whole story. Somehow, whatever Ryan had done, she couldn't believe he was a criminal at heart. 'And I'm neither skittish nor a virgin,' she added belatedly.

'Well, then?'

Angela closed her eyes and let her chin drop on to her chest. She couldn't think clearly when Ryan was this close, watching her with that astute, unswerving gaze, and with his big hands holding her, making her whole body come tinglingly alive . . .

'Go on,' he insisted, sliding one of those hands to the nape of her neck, and holding her so that she couldn't look away.

Help! He wasn't going to let her put him off.

'It's just . . . ' She tried again, searching for the words to tell him . . . to tell him . . . what? That she was content with her life the way it was? That she found it busy and satisfying and didn't want anything to change it? No, she couldn't tell him that. Because it wasn't true — hadn't been true for some time. Even before Ryan came to town, she had been conscious of a certain restlessness, an intuition that the time had come for change.

And now, here in her own house, with Al sleeping peacefully in his cage, and Ryan's hands on her as if he thought she might try to slip away, she could no longer avoid the knowledge that something unexpected had happened. It wasn't just that she found Ryan overwhelmingly attractive. That, after all, was hardly surprising. He was an exceptionally gorgeous hunk of man. But there was more to it than that. A tenderness, a feeling of wonder, and a tenuous empathy that she'd never experienced before. Certainly not with Kelvin, the husband she had once so dearly loved.

She closed her eyes. Was it possible that she, Angela Baddingley, after twelve years of happily unwedded bliss, had once again become the target of Cupid's arrow? She'd been so sure it couldn't happen. *Shouldn't* happen with a man like Ryan, who looked on lovemaking as . . . what had he called it? . . . 'a moment of passion and closeness stolen from the solitude of life'? A strong, disciplined sort of man, shaped by circumstances she might never understand.

Surely, if she gave herself to him now, heartbreak would inevitably follow.

She opened her eyes again. He was watching her with a small furrow between his brows, and the lines around his mouth were deeply grooved, His skin, so firm and golden for a man who spent a lot of his time indoors, looked soft and strokable as satin.

Slowly, not meaning to, she raised her arm and ran the tips of her fingers across his cheek.

Ryan caught her wrist and pressed his lips to her palm. Then, still holding her firmly, he looked up and said, 'Well?'

'I don't know.' Angela gazed vacantly round the room, seeking an answer she knew would only be found in her heart. 'It's true my libido is — normal. But, Ryan, I'm not looking for trouble. When I dropped that jacket I only meant it as a joke . . . '

'Some joke,' he muttered, releasing her abruptly, and throwing himself against the back of the sofa. 'But you're right, of course. I am trouble.'

He looked her straight in the eye, and gave her a smile of such sensuous, blatant challenge that she found herself digging her nails into the cushions. Dear heaven, how gloriously male he looked, sprawled there in his elegant suit as if he alone in Caley Cove was totally immune to the heat. Gloriously male, and utterly irresistible.

But as she struggled to find words, with no warning he rose to his feet.

'Well, that's that, then,' he said matter-of-factly, 'Thanks for the coffee.'

She stared at him, not really believing, because there was something in the calm grey gaze that belied his careless dismissal. And as he started to move away from her, Angela knew she couldn't let him go. Not like this. She reached out to catch on to his hand.

'Ryan, wait . . . '

He stopped, stood for a moment with his back to her, then turned round slowly, and gazed down into her eyes. After a while he shook his head, said, 'For Pete's sake, Angela, make up what's left of your mind,' and hauled her on to her feet and into his arms.

Peace. Not passion at first, but peace. A great sensuous lethargy. A feeling that she was where she belonged. 'There's nothing wrong with my mind,' she murmured into the smooth white silk of his shirt. 'It's just that I didn't mean this to happen. You — you sort of snuck up on me when I still thought you were an arrogant jackass.'

'Nothing *has* happened yet,' he pointed out. 'And I am an arrogant jackass. You'd be well-advised not to forget it.' As he spoke, the palm of his hand moved purposefully down to her waist.

Angela gave a small, contented sigh, and gave up trying to fight this thing that hadn't yet happened. She rubbed her cheek against his chest. He smelled so clean and warm and male, and just being here in his arms felt so right that it was hard to remember it was probably all wrong.

She wrapped her arms around him and ran her hands over the dark fabric of his trousers, revelling in the solid strength of his hips and thighs. Maybe she was crazy — she had to be — but she couldn't help it, because suddenly — or maybe not so suddenly — she was aware that the calm, fulfilling days of her uneventful life hadn't been as fulfilling as she'd thought. She wanted more now. And the more that she wanted was Ryan. Now, in her own small bed. And be damned to the future.

She gave a small sigh of pleasure and lifted her lips for his kiss. He took them with a hard, hungry passion that ignited such an explosion of desire that she expected to burst into flames at any moment. She moved rapturously against his body, offering herself with uninhibited ardour.

But, incredibly, she heard his indrawn breath, realised with stunned bewilderment that he was forcing himself to exercise an iron control. Why? Why was he drawing back, seeming to hesitate?

'Ryan?' She raised her eyes, felt his fingers tangle in her hair and pull her head back. He stared down at her then for a long, endless moment, studying every angle, every shadow that crossed her features, even turning her face to catch the light.

'Hell,' he said, so roughly that she jumped. 'Angela, this isn't going to work.'

'Why?' She blinked at him, dazed and open-mouthed. 'Ryan, it's all right.' It had to be all right. Somehow his hands had shifted to her hips, and he was stroking the silk of her dress, holding her against him so that she could feel his need which was as great as her own.

'Ryan, I *was* behaving like a skittish virgin but . . . ' Then the feel of him, the knowledge that for some reason she was losing him, made her slide her hands around his waist until she found the buckle of his belt.

Ryan swore, and reached down to grab her wrists. 'No,' he said, in a tone so harsh it made her flinch. 'You were right the first time. I should have seen what was happening. And you weren't being skittish, you were being sensible. Keeping out of trouble. Which is more than I can say for myself.'

'I think,' said Angela, gazing at the rise and fall of muscles across his chest, 'that I've changed my mind about sense.'

'What's that supposed to mean?' He spoke so coldly, she wanted to cry.

She forced herself to reply lightly. 'That — that if you're still open to offers I might not be averse to a bit of trouble.' She took a deep breath. 'After all, what do I really have to lose?' She pulled out of his grasp, put her hands behind her back and smiled up at him — a soft, hungry, sultry smile so explicit that he couldn't miss the invitation. She didn't know why he suddenly needed an invitation, but she did know she couldn't bear this yearning ache in her body for a moment longer. Tomorrow she might regret it. Now, in the loneliness of the night, nothing mattered but the virile man gazing down at her out of smoky, half-hooded grey eyes.

'No!' The word exploded out of him like shrapnel.

Angela felt something cold and heavy plummet to the pit of her stomach. 'What is it?' she whispered. 'I thought — I thought that was what you wanted.'

'It was.' The skin was pulled tight across his cheekbones, and there was a hardness in his eyes now that, for the first time, made Angela believe he might have been capable of murder. 'It's not any more.' His lips parted in a travesty of a smile, and he lifted a hand and touched his knuckles to her cheek.

'A lucky escape for you this time. Sleep well, Angela, darling.'

'Ryan!' she cried out as he swung away from her. 'Don't call me your darling and then . . . Listen, I know I said some things I didn't mean, but — '

'There aren't any buts.' He stopped, and when he looked back over his shoulder she couldn't detect even a trace of affection in his eyes. 'You know, Angel, for a grown woman, you can be remarkably dim-witted.'

'Oh! Of all the . . . ' She stopped.

Ryan was right about that much at least. She had known all along that giving in to him could only bring disaster. And, just because she had suddenly been overtaken by the most blatant and searing attack of lust she had ever known, that was no reason to take leave of her senses.

Imagine sensible Angela Baddingley having Ryan Koniski to thank for saving her from a fate much more stimulating than death. A fate, though, she admitted, which might have made it impossible for her to carry on with her ordinary, uneventful life in Caley Cove. She had a feeling that after Ryan ordinary and uneventful would come very low on her scale of priorities. Long after exciting, exhilarating and alive . . .

She took a long breath and gazed at the tall man who was now standing silently by the door. Al stirred in his cage, an owl hooted softly in the night, and a smile touched Ryan's lips, hovered there for a second and was gone. It was a strange smile. Twisted with a bitter regret she couldn't even begin to comprehend. She watched him, not saying anything, and after a while he murmured something under his breath and moved back into the room. Then he took her face in his hands, kissed her oh, so lightly on the forehead, and let her go.

Angela closed her eyes, hoping that somehow this nightmare would turn out to be a dream. But a moment later she heard the front door close gently, followed by the loud crunch of Ryan's feet on the gravel.

By the time she reached the front of the house, the lights of the Alfa-Romeo were already receding down the road.

★   ★   ★

'Hi, Charlotte. It was kind of you to invite me. How's Harry?'

'Harry's doing nicely, dear. He's gone to help Rob look for a place of his own. Such a nice boy. I'll miss him. Now you come on in and have that nice cup of tea I promised you. I've made my lemon sponge specially for you.'

Angela followed Charlotte's steel-grey bun into the Koniski sitting-room and reminded herself that she mustn't think about the last time she had been here. She mustn't think about Ryan at all. She wouldn't have come today if Charlotte hadn't phoned her up and insisted she collect her rain-check on the tea that Ryan hadn't provided on that memorable day. Ryan, she remembered bitterly, had provided kisses instead — and now he'd gone back to Seattle. And she was back in this house that held too many memories.

Stop it, Angela, she told herself. She smiled brightly at Charlotte and said wasn't it about time they had some rain?

'Yes, dear,' agreed Charlotte, busy slicing the cake. 'But it was perfect on the night of the ball. Don't you think so? Hard to believe that was a week ago, isn't it?'

'Yes,' agreed Angela neutrally. 'The time has gone by fast.'

In fact it had crawled by, as she had tried hopelessly to put the events of the ball and its aftermath in perspective. Surely that night had been no more than a moment of summer madness that had passed. Sometimes she wondered again if she was in love with Ryan Koniski, but in her saner moments she knew that couldn't be so. Why, she hardly knew him. And anyway, what was love beyond an atavistic and inconvenient instinct that made foolish men and women seek a mate? Ryan had come to that conclusion long ago. It was the only reason she could think of for his abrupt departure when she was just about to give him what he wanted. He must have read her susceptibility in her eyes, and decided she might become an encumbrance instead of just a casual frolic in the night.

But if she *didn't* love him — or if love was only blind instinct — why did her life, which had once been so full and contented, now seem so dreary and pointless? And why was she moping round the office looking, as Rob had unkindly put it, like last week's left-over cabbage?

Charlotte poured the tea, patted her hair, and asked gently, 'Did you enjoy the ball, dear?'

'Yes, very much.'

Her hostess cleared her throat. 'I think my nephew did too. He's had a difficult time of it, you know.'

'Yes,' said Angela. 'I heard.'

'Oh.' For a moment Charlotte looked nonplussed. Then she brightened and said decisively, 'But he really is a very nice boy.'

'Yes.' Lord, how long was this going to go on? What was Ryan's devoted aunt up to? What did she think she could possibly achieve by harping on about her nephew and the ball? Angela glanced round the room, searching for something to talk about that couldn't be connected with Ryan.

'That's an interesting — um — umbrella stand,' she murmured, pointing to a bullet-shaped brass container beneath the window.

'What? Oh, that's a sculpture, dear. Harry bought it at an auction in Seattle. I think it's supposed to symbolise man's brain, but Ryan says it looks more like man's ... ' She stopped, cleared her throat, and finished hastily, 'Er — digestive system.'

Angela choked, tried not to laugh, and then found she didn't want to after all. Ryan had always had the power to make her laugh, even at his most inflexible and reserved, but just now she couldn't bear to think about him.

'Ryan's busy with a nice case of assault with a deadly boot,' continued Charlotte cosily, oblivious to the glazed distress in her guest's eye. 'But then he's always busy. You *do* like him, don't you, dear?'

'Yes, of course.' Angela swallowed her cake and washed it down with the last of her tea. 'That was delicious, Charlotte, but I'm afraid I have to be going ... ' She braced herself, half expecting her hostess to protest.

But to her surprise Charlotte's face lit up and her gaze slanted brightly towards the window. When Angela turned her head, she heard the sound of a car throbbing to a halt in the driveway.

Harry and Rob must have returned.

But it wasn't Harry, or Rob, who walked through the doorway a moment later and held her motionless in a hard grey gaze.

It was Ryan. He was carrying a suitcase. Dressed in trousers and a white cotton shirt, he looked coolly prepared to spend the weekend.

7

Angela grabbed for her plate, which was about to slide off her pink summer skirt on to the carpet. She opened her mouth, realised no sound was coming out, and quickly closed it.

'Hello, Angela. Aunt Charlotte.' Ryan put his suitcase on the floor and walked across the room to kiss his aunt. 'I see you've made my favourite lemon sponge.'

'Yes, dear. I made it for Angela. But I hoped you'd be here in time for tea.'

Ryan's eyes narrowed. 'Hoped? Aunt Charlotte, you knew I'd be here. You called me to say you were worried about Dad's health — '

'Well, yes, dear. Your father did look a little pale this morning, and I knew it would cheer him up to see you.'

'Aunt Charlotte . . . ' Ryan sank on to the nearest flat surface, a red brocade chair with wooden arms carved into bird claws. 'Do you mean to tell me you got me to rearrange my schedule in the middle of an important case and come all the way out here just because Dad looked *pale*?'

'It's good for you to get away, dear,' said Charlotte, smiling comfortably from the depths of her armchair. She threw a meaningful glance Angela's way.

Ryan followed the direction of her eyes, and encountered Angela's stony stare and tightly set mouth. The light, or part of it, appeared to dawn on both of them at the same moment.

'Charlotte, you didn't . . . '

'Angela, if this was your idea . . . ?'

'It wasn't,' said Angela, regaining the use of her limbs and standing up. 'Thank you, Charlotte. The cake was delicious. Goodbye, Ryan, I hope you have a pleasant weekend.' She spun round, ignoring her hostess's vague twitterings, and practically ran out of the room.

'Charlotte, how could you?' Angela groaned out loud as a loose pebble from the path shot up and hit her on the leg. 'I know you meant well, but . . . ' She swallowed the rest of her sentence when she saw Molly Bracken from the post office eyeing her curiously from the other side of the street.

Oh, of course Ryan's devoted aunt meant well. She ran distracted fingers through her hair. Charlotte loved her nephew, and apparently had some foolish notion that he needed a mate. But to summon him from Seattle on a trumped-up excuse about Harry's health, and to arrange this patently obvious chance meeting over a lemon sponge cake . . . it was too much. Ryan had been angry, although he'd tried not to show it. And she . . . she was merely devastated.

I'd no idea, she thought dazedly, dashing the back of her hand across her eyes. No idea that seeing him again could hurt so much. She stumbled over a crack in the pavement, and tugged blindly at the door of her car.

It wasn't until she was already seated behind the wheel that she realised something wasn't quite right. Just before she got in, hadn't she noticed . . . ?

Grumbling under her breath, she climbed out again and bent to look at her left front tyre.

It was flat. So flat it was only fit for decent burial.

'Damn,' she muttered, biting her lip. As if things weren't bad enough already, she was about to provide a sideshow for the neighbours. As well as Ryan, if he happened to be looking. She could just see the item in the Caley Cove *Courier* if they turned out to be short of news tomorrow. LOCAL ATTORNEY MAKES INCOMPETENT ATTEMPT TO CHANGE TYRE. All right, maybe they wouldn't be quite that desperate for news. Or that unkind. She kicked glumly at the offending wheel. She'd never been much good at things mechanical, and although she would eventually get the job done she'd probably end up with more grease on herself than on the car. Unless she went back into the house to ask for help . . .

'I won't do it,' she announced firmly. 'I'll just have to manage on my own.'

'Commendably liberated,' Ryan's voice drawled softly from behind her. 'Can I watch?'

Angela whirled round to find him standing relaxed and cat-like against the gatepost, with his hands in his pockets and his mouth twisted into something that wasn't quite a sneer. It wasn't a smile either. But just seeing him there, all loose-limbed and casual, yet with that air of watchfulness that seemed to be a part of his makeup, was enough to make a lump catch in the back of her throat.

'No,' she said. 'You can't watch.' A curtain twitched in a house across the road, and she added grimly, 'Your neighbours have the situation covered.'

'I don't doubt it. Do you want a hand?'

She did, very much, but she certainly

didn't want to admit it. 'No, thank you,' she said.

He nodded, and settled himself more comfortably against the gatepost. 'Fine.'

Lifting her chin, Angela marched to the back of the car and removed the spare. Ryan began to whistle through his teeth as she pulled out the jack and set it down on the pavement.

'I said you can't watch,' she snapped.

'So try and stop me.'

Angela flung round with her hands on her hips. 'Go *away*.' She was practically spitting at him. 'Haven't you done enough already? Do you have to humiliate me as well?'

He straightened, the expression on his face no longer softly mocking, but austere and unreadable as rock. 'I offered to help,' he said evenly. 'As for humiliating you — surely you did that to yourself.'

'What do you mean?'

'This little plot you cooked up with Aunt Charlotte.'

'Oh!' Angela gasped. Rage at the

undeserved accusation steamed through her and made her raise her hand.

'I wouldn't,' he said mildly. 'I learned the hard way how not to take abuse. And I fight dirty.'

'I *bet* you do,' she muttered. But she lowered her arm, and as she did so she caught sight of Charlotte's face peering anxiously through the front window.

'That's better,' he said. 'Now — '

'Now,' said Angela through clenched teeth, 'I'd like to make it clear to you, you arrogant — '

'Jackass,' he finished for her. 'That's the one I like best.'

She breathed in hard. 'I'd like to make it clear that I had no idea you were coming home this weekend. If I had known, I wouldn't have accepted Charlotte's invitation.'

'Hmm.' His unblinking grey gaze stayed on her face for so long that she felt as if he was pinning her to the car. She heard a bee buzz gently in the hollyhocks by the gate.

After a while she asked him, 'Why on

earth should I go out of my way to . . . ?' She had been going to say 'torture myself'. But in the end pride wouldn't let her. 'To see a man who doesn't even want me?'

'Oh, I want you,' he said, almost conversationally.

'Sure. When, and if, it ever happens to suit you. And then only for a weekend.'

'Or two.' His eyes mocked her. 'OK, let's agree that Aunt Charlotte is to blame for this fiasco, and get on with fixing your tyre. After which I can get back to my client with the deadly boot and you can get back to your dilapidated bird.'

'You can get back to your damned boot right this minute,' Angela snapped. 'I don't need your help.'

'Fine.' He gave her a look that left her wondering if he wanted to slap her or kiss her, and returned to the house without doing either.

By the time Angela climbed into her car half an hour later, the pain she'd felt at seeing Ryan again had been subli-mated by a flaming indignation. But the tyre had been successfully changed and her pink skirt was streaked with road dirt and grease.

As she pulled away, she tried not to look back at the house, but she couldn't stop herself.

She needn't have worried. Ryan's face was not in the window. Neither, surprisingly, was Charlotte's.

★ ★ ★

Monday was busier than usual at the office, partly because she had given Rob the day off to move into his new apartment. Angela was glad of the extra work. It kept her mind off Ryan and that ridiculous scene outside his father's house. Had he been laughing at her as she bumbled around changing the tyre? If he had, she couldn't blame him. He'd offered to help, and she'd turned him down out of sheer bloody-mindedness.

He hadn't seemed to be laughing,

though, she remembered. *She* hadn't been laughing either. The ache behind her eyes, and the sense of life's total futility, was not even remotely amusing.

By the time Monday came to an end, Angela was sticky from the heat and anxious for a long, cool shower. She was also tired, hungry and anti-social. It was too hot to exercise, and all she wanted was a quiet evening alone with Al and a book. As a result, she was anything but pleased to hear a car door slam and the sound of brisk footsteps on the driveway just as she was clearing salad and cheese from her patio table. She'd been looking forward to basking peacefully in the breeze off the water.

Scowling, she tugged her T-shirt down over the waistband of her shorts and moved reluctantly to answer the door.

'Hello, dear. I am sorry to bother you. But I could see you and Ryan weren't a bit pleased with me the other day, and I just felt I had to explain.' Charlotte stood on the doorstep bobbing her head up and down and looked like a guilty mother hen.

'There's nothing to explain,' said Angela. There was, but she didn't much care.

'I'm afraid there is, dear. May I come in?'

'Oh. Of course.' Angela stood aside without enthusiasm and watched glumly as Charlotte marched straight into the living-room and settled into a sturdy tweed chair.

'I won't stay long,' she said, clasping pudgy hands in her lap. 'Don't bother making me tea.'

Angela hadn't intended to. She stared at a cluster of bright buttercups on the lawn and waited for her unwanted guest to explain her visit.

'It's about Ryan,' said Charlotte.

'Yes.' Angela sat on the love-seat and crossed one knee over the other. Of course it was about Ryan. Everything was about Ryan. She gritted her teeth and hoped her eyes weren't as glittery as they felt.

'He really is a very nice boy. He

hasn't had a happy life, you see.'

'No. I suppose he hasn't.'

'Oh, I don't just mean that awful business . . . ' Charlotte stopped and blew her nose suddenly. 'You see, it started long before that.'

'What did?' asked Angela bluntly. At this rate Charlotte would still be here fidgeting with her hair and blowing her nose at midnight.

'Well, you see, Ryan's mother died when he was born. Such a nice girl, Laura. And I'm afraid my poor Harry didn't think a son was much compensation at the time. Later, when he'd got over it a bit, he started to pin all his hopes and dreams on little Ryan.' She heaved a gusty sigh. 'But he was a difficult child.'

'I can imagine,' said Angela drily, wondering what his aunt thought Ryan's childhood could possibly have to do with her.

'Yes. Wilful. Always knew what he wanted, but if he thought his father might approve he wanted the opposite.

I think he knew — well, that if he hadn't arrived on the scene his mother would still be alive. And he guessed Harry found that hard to forget. He was a very bright boy. Harry wanted him to be a nice doctor.'

'Huh. Great beside manner,' muttered Angela.

Charlotte blinked doubtfully. 'I know he seems a little — cantankerous sometimes. But, Angela, dear, life hasn't been kind to him, you know. And he grew up with so much expected of him that, given the sort of boy he used to be, he was bound to resent it — and fight back the only way he knew how, by refusing to co-operate with his father. I'm sure that's why he made those awful friends. And Harry — Harry couldn't understand — didn't try very hard, I'm afraid.' She swallowed, and Angela could see the muscles working in her throat. 'Then when Ryan got into trouble with the local police — nothing too serious, mind you — Harry washed his hands of him instead of trying to find out what was wrong. Of course, the nice people here in Caley Cove took Harry's side, and most of them turned their backs on Ryan too. So he moved to Seattle. That's when he got into real trouble.' Charlotte smiled nervously and looked away.

Angela uncrossed her legs, breathed deeply, and wriggled her shoulders. She still didn't see what any of this had to do with her. But, as it had to do with Ryan, however hard she tried, she couldn't pretend she didn't care.

'He always had you, didn't he?' she murmured. 'You tried to help.'

'Of course I did. I brought him up, you see. But I've never had much money of my own, and — well, when the court case came up Harry refused to pay for a lawyer. Refused to have anything to do with his own son. He was hurting too — of course he was, but . . . ' Charlotte paused to dab a tissue at her eyes. 'But Ryan didn't see it that way. He felt his father had let him down when he needed him most because he didn't — didn't give a damn about him, is what he said. For a long time it made him very bitter.'

'Having a son charged with manslaughter is kind of a let-down too,' observed Angela, who no longer knew whose side she was on, and wasn't even sure it mattered. In a way, it sounded as though both Koniski men had had reason to hold something of a grudge.

Charlotte twisted the tissue into a wad, and her head drooped. 'That's just it. But if Ryan had had a good lawyer, instead of that overworked young man the courts appointed, he might very well not have gone to prison.'

'Oh!' exclaimed Angela. 'Is *that* what happened? No wonder he's so bitter about it.'

'He *has* forgiven Harry, though,' Charlotte hastened to assure her. 'He knows he was partly to blame.'

Yes, that was exactly the impression Angela had formed — along with a strong sense that Ryan was too obstinately proud for his own good. His refusal to clear his name — assuming he could — had to be more than just a reluctance to fight the system. He was a born fighter, so unless there was something she didn't know about . . .

But of course there was plenty she didn't know. Ryan had really told her very little.

'What happened that night?' she asked Charlotte, half afraid to hear the answer.

She needn't have worried. When the older woman lifted her face, it was damp and shining with tears. 'I'm not sure, dear. Harry wouldn't let me attend the trial. He didn't go either, so poor Ryan had to bear it all alone. And he won't talk about it. But I do know it wasn't his fault. I could tell you — no, he said I mustn't, that it would make him sound like a holy martyr. Which he insists he's not.'

She tightened her mouth, and Angela wondered how on earth Ryan had succeeded in sealing lips that were normally unsealable. Perhaps it was just that his aunt loved him very much.

'I see,' she said, not seeing at all. Al, who had been asleep on top of his cage, gave a soft 'grack' and she went to lift him on to her shoulder.

'I was sure you'd understand,' said Charlotte, nodding. 'Ryan started studying law while he was in prison, you know, and now he's always taking on cases involving young people who've got themselves in trouble. Like the young man he's defending now, who broke his boss's nose with a work boot.'

'Oh,' said Angela faintly, wondering why Ryan considered that particular paragon worth defending.

'Yes.' Unexpectedly Charlotte moved in for the kill. 'So you see, my dear, Ryan really does need someone to look after him. A wife. That's why I invited you to tea.'

Angela managed not to blink. Ryan needed a wife about as much as she needed a pet python. Fortunately, Al chose that moment to peck her ear, giving her the opportunity to let out a legitimate screech. 'Charlotte,' she finally gasped, 'are you suggesting I ought to rush off and offer to — um — marry Ryan? Don't you know that even if I wanted to, which I don't, he'd turn me down?'

'Yes, I expect he would, dear. He's always insisted on making his own moves. But I'm sure he cares about you, and I can tell you care about him.'

'Yes, but, Charlotte, I don't *want* to get married,' Angela groaned. 'I'm extremely happily divorced.'

'Yes, dear, I'm sure you are. And Ryan says he's very happily single. Well, now that we've got that settled . . . ' Charlotte beamed at Angela, as if she'd been given exactly the response she wanted and was already setting dates and ordering flowers. Then she stood up and announced firmly, 'Now it really is time I was going.'

Angela was still standing in the middle of her living-room, gaping, when she heard the door shut. She shook her head and collapsed into the nearest chair. Had Charlotte Koniski taken leave of her senses? Or had she?

After a while, as Al nibbled gently on her ear, she ceased to worry about the state of Charlotte's psyche, and began to brood about her own.

Why had she sat there listening to Charlotte, and avidly gleaning every crumb of information about her nephew that his fond aunt had been willing to impart? It was as if she . . . No. Oh, no. She'd already been over all that, and she *couldn't* have fallen in love again after all these years. Not with anyone. And certainly not with Ryan.

But of course she had. That, she realised in one stupefying flash of enlightenment, was the whole trouble.

Angela dropped her head into her hands and gave a shudder that made Al natter crossly. And to think she hadn't even seen it coming. Not really. Oh, she'd known almost from the beginning that she wanted Ryan, but she hadn't believed it when wanting had turned

189

gradually into love. But Charlotte had seen — seen that there was at least one woman who, in spite of all her protestations to the contrary, was misguided enough to want to look after a man who would accept about as much looking after as your average lion. Only Charlotte didn't understand that Ryan would never care about a lasting commitment. He had been crushingly forthright about that — and she had whole-heartedly agreed with him. Why, even the thought of serious involvement had brought back painful memories of Kelvin, made her want to turn tail and run. So it was probably just as well that Charlotte wasn't likely to get her way.

It didn't feel just as well, though. It felt — as if she'd been shown a glimpse of the gates of paradise, only to be told she'd never enter.

Angela's mouth twisted painfully. She could understand well enough why Ryan chose to live strictly in the present. His past, after all, was best forgotten. And the future — well, he'd thought he had a future once before. And it had been stolen from him, or perhaps he had thrown it away one night in front of a pool hall in Seattle. And why Charlotte thought she, Angela, could change him was beyond her.

'Why did she have to come here, Al?' she whispered to the oblivious little bird. 'I *was* getting on with getting over him. Wasn't I?'

The following evening Angela learned the answer to the first part of her question. And she wished she hadn't.

She was sitting on the patio watching the buttercups do their dance on the lawn, and not wanting to think about mowing because they were so pretty and yellow, when she heard the phone ring. She ran into the kitchen to pick it up.

'Angela?' enquired a clipped and irate voice on the other end.

Her heart jumped, then felt as if it was skidding to a stop. And who did he *think* she was? Al?

'Hello, Ryan,' she said warily.

'Don't sound so delighted,' he snapped.

'Should I be?'

There was a long pause during which she could almost hear him counting to ten. Then he sighed and replied wearily, 'No. Not if Aunt Charlotte's been as busy arranging your life as she has mine. Has she, by any chance, been to see you?'

'Yes. She told me you were really a very nice boy.'

'She told me *you* were a lovely girl who needed to settle down and start a family.'

'Ouch. Help!'

'That's what I thought. She phoned me a few minutes ago and said she needs me to look over her will. No later than next weekend. I told her that was more in your line, but she insisted that I was family, and she'd just been to see Dr Colombo and — '

'Is she ill?'

'I doubt it. But if I'm not mistaken,

unless she gets her way, she has every intention of spending the next few months being fragile. Which will be very hard on Dad. Given his heart condition, he doesn't need that kind of worry.'

No, he probably didn't. But did Ryan have to make it sound as if he blamed his aunt's precarious state of health on her?

'I don't see the problem,' she said briskly, determined not to let him know what the sound of his voice was doing to her pulse-rate. 'And anyway I'm sure Charlotte wouldn't — '

'Oh, yes, she would. She's done it before once or twice. When I was in prison, for instance. Dad kept her from attending the trial, but when he tried to stop her coming to visit me she retired to bed. The doctor said she was in a very bad way. So Dad was forced to give in.'

'I don't understand. Surely if there's nothing wrong with your aunt — '

'You don't know Aunt Charlotte,'

Ryan interrupted grimly. 'There will be plenty wrong with her by the time she's worked herself into the part. She's always had a talent for putting mind over matter.' He sighed. 'All for our own good, mind you.'

'Oh, dear.' Angela decided there wasn't much point in trying to make sense out of nonsense.

'Is that all you can say?' Ryan didn't try to hide his impatience.

She could think of a lot of things, none of them remotely complimentary. 'No,' she said, yanking open a cupboard door and slamming it loudly enough for him to hear. 'Dammit, she's your . . . '

Angela stopped. She had been about to say 'she's your aunt'. But she was fond of that wily old woman, and, even though Ryan wasn't making a lot of sense, if there was anything she could do to keep Charlotte well . . .

'What do you suggest?' she asked resignedly.

This time he was silent for so long that she wondered if he'd hung up, but eventually he replied in a flat, unemotional voice, 'Angela, this case I'm working on is much more complicated than I thought. The fact is, right now I just don't have time to cope with Aunt Charlotte's little schemes.'

'And you think I have?' If he hadn't been in Seattle, Angela would have picked up the nearest blunt object and thrown it at him. Her gaze strayed round the kitchen. The nearest object was a big copper canister filled with sugar.

'No, I don't think you have,' he said curtly. 'I doubt if either one of us has. That's why I'm suggesting you go round to see her and convince her that she might as well stay healthy.'

'How? I don't see — '

'For heaven's sake. Just add your voice to mine and explain. That ought to do it.'

Angela stared into the mouthpiece and twisted the cord round her wrist. 'What are you talking about?' she demanded, pulling a white wooden chair away from the table. 'Do what? Explain what?'

'About our engagement.' He sounded bored and very slightly defensive. 'Don't you get it? Aunt Charlotte is plotting holy deadlock. With two charming children to follow. Presumably in that order.'

8

'What?' Angela rubbed her ear, instinctively assuming she'd misheard.

'I said Aunt Charlotte wants us to get engaged.' Ryan's reply was curt, but not to the point of rudeness.

'That's what I thought you said.' She lowered herself carefully into the chair and waited for him to go on. When he didn't, she said, 'I already know what Charlotte has in mind. The point is, what do *you* want?'

There was another long silence, and finally he said, 'You,' almost as if it came as a surprise.

'Me?' she just managed to keep her voice level. 'You didn't tell Charlotte — '

'I told her I'd think about it. So if you'd just drop in on her and smooth her down — let her know that our engagement — '

'What engagement?' Angela found

herself grinding her molars. 'Ryan, you can think about it all you like, but even Kelvin managed to propose to me in person, and if you imagine I'm getting engaged to you just because you have a problem with *your* aunt and *your* work schedule it's my pleasure to tell you it isn't going to happen.'

'Is that so? Listen, Angela, I've had one helluva day — '

'So have I,' said Angela, and hung up.

For a while she sat totally still, staring at the silent phone and half expecting to hear it ring again. When it didn't, she switched her gaze to the copper canister and entertained herself with fantasies of emptying its contents over Ryan Koniski's head, along with a liberal libation of water. He could do with a little sweetening up, she thought viciously.

But very soon the improbable fantasies ceased to provide consolation, and she was forced to face the fact that she had just turned down the only offer of marriage she was ever likely to receive from the man she loved. If it *had* been an offer. Now that she thought about it, he hadn't actually asked her to marry him. He had said he wanted her, but not as if he wanted to want her. Of course it was quite possible that he was thinking in terms of a temporary engagement as a way of legitimising lust, and conveniently placating his aunt. But as a genuine preliminary to marriage? Surely not.

'You don't want marriage, Angela,' she reminded herself. 'You've already been there, and it didn't work.'

She put her elbows on the table and buried her face in her hands. No, she didn't want marriage, but, strangely, since meeting Ryan she had become aware that often her own company wasn't enough. And she had become achingly conscious of bodily hungers that hadn't worried her overmuch for years. Sometimes she even thought nostalgically of the children she now would never have. But maybe she could still hope for something . . . something loving, and tender and close . . .

'With Ryan Koniski? Angela Baddingley, you are very definitely out of your mind.' She sat up suddenly and saw the heart-shaped leaves of a black cottonwood move gently in the breeze outside her window. Then she jumped to her feet to start chopping vegetables for supper.

'Arrogant, self-satisfied man,' she muttered, slicing a stick of celery in half. 'So you think I can just pop over and smooth down Charlotte for you, do you? And get engaged to you if it happens to suit you. Just like that.' She stabbed a tomato and the juice spurted over the counter. 'Well, Mr Koniski, you can think again.' A bunch of carrots was reduced to chips. 'And you can solve your own damn problems.' Her knife slipped and she cut her little finger and swore.

Over a hundred miles away, in a bright and spacious office close to downtown Seattle, Ryan was also swearing, but with an imagery and imagination that the cause of his frustration couldn't equal.

'Damn the woman,' he finished tightly, when he finally ran out of inspiration.

'What woman? Not that small-town lawyer you've been pursuing?' Martin Cody, his partner and long-time friend, glanced at Ryan with a mixture of amusement and disbelief. 'I thought you'd decided to give her a break.'

'What's that supposed to mean?' Ryan had himself in control, but he looked as menacing as Martin had ever seen him. And his grey eyes were narrow with a dawning purpose that didn't bode well for the woman who had evoked this uncharacteristic explosion of profanity.

'Well,' replied Martin carefully, 'I've noticed that normally when you find yourself involved with a heart that's in danger of breaking you leave before the damage is irreversible. I thought you didn't want to hurt this particular lady.'

'I didn't. I've changed my mind.'

The sound of Ryan's hand slapping

the hard surface of his desk made Martin jump. 'That's not like you,' he said mildly.

'Isn't it?' Ryan pushed his chair back and smiled grimly. 'Don't worry, I'm not going to beat her. But it seems I made quite a mistake. Ms Baddingley is a lot tougher than I thought. So, I believe, is her heart.'

Martin shrugged. 'Is it? That ought to make things easier.'

'That's what I thought.' Ryan stared at a row of law books on a shelf and imagined Angela standing in her living-room informing that misbegotten bird that she'd just hung up the phone on Ryan Koniski.

His lips flattened. Where had he ever got the idea that she might care for him a little too much? That he might have discovered a woman misguided enough to think she could forget about his past? The kind of woman, in fact, whom he had long ago decided to avoid, because, as Martin had said, he wasn't in the business of breaking hearts.

There had once been a time, though, before Connie and before Amy, when he had dreamed . . .

No. He pulled himself back to the present. Dreams were for sleeping, not for the neon reality of day. Impatiently, ignoring the affectionate understanding in Martin's eyes, he picked up a pencil and began to draw straight, bar-like lines down a sheet of paper. Yes, there had been a time. But that was long ago, before he had fully confronted the burden of his past.

He drew a dark, heavy circle around the lines, broke his pencil, and tossed it irritably down on the desk. Of course, he should have seen that only Angela's pride had been wounded when he'd refused to take advantage of the undeniable chemistry between them. She had assured him her heart wasn't involved. He should have believed her. Women didn't hang up phones on men who mattered to them.

Oh, sure, he'd been a little abrupt when he'd called her just now, but she ought to know he hadn't time to play games . . .

The sound of Martin clearing his throat brought Ryan's mind smartly back to the office. He had deadlines to meet and promises to keep which couldn't be put off for Ms Baddingley. But come the weekend perhaps he would find time for a bit of game-playing. Game-playing of a very specific nature.

He looked across at his partner and arched his eyebrows. 'My small-town lawyer is in for a surprise,' he announced with a lightness that didn't deceive Martin for a moment. 'I'm beginning to look forward to it. Do you know, I do believe I've missed Ms Angela Baddingley?'

* * *

By the following morning Angela had recovered from her fit of temper, and was suffering from a vague sense of disappointment — along with a bodily ache that wasn't vague at all. Although she knew she was being contrary, she realised she had expected Ryan to pick up the phone at once and call her back.

He hadn't.

'Not that I wanted him to,' she assured Al, who was watching her top a boiled egg. 'But if he had, I'd have enjoyed giving him a piece of my mind.'

The rest of the week passed slowly. Rob was back at work, and because it was summer a number of her clients were away. Ryan still didn't call and, somewhat to Angela's surprise, neither did Charlotte. Presumably Ryan had exaggerated the problem with his aunt. She felt relieved, and yet oddly unsettled, and plunged herself into a furious reorganisation of her files which left her feeling hot, damp and dissatisfied.

On Saturday she decided to dig a new flowerbed, which made her even damper and hotter, but it saved her from having to think.

She was slumped over her shovel,

taking a break and breathing rapidly in the sultry summer air, when a glimmer of gold caught her eye. She glanced towards the fence. Ryan was leaning on it, the midday sun glinting off his tawny mane of hair.

Their eyes met, hers guarded, his, if she was not mistaken, bright with retaliatory intent.

Neither of them spoke for a moment, and then Ryan said, 'OK. You wanted me in person. You've got me.'

Angela said, 'Why?'

'Among other things, because I don't like being hung up on.'

'Then I'd suggest you don't go around telling people you expect them to get engaged to you because you happen to be overloaded with work. Especially I wouldn't tell them that over the phone.'

'I didn't,' he said shortly. 'I was trying to explain that I needed you to dampen Aunt Charlotte's enthusiasm, persuade her a wedding was in nobody's best interests, and somehow convince her that our engagement was off — '

'It was never on.'

'As a matter of fact, that hadn't escaped my notice. It probably hadn't escaped Aunt Charlotte's either, but that hasn't stopped her from convincing herself our union is written in the stars. All I was asking you to do was help me make her face up to reality. I'd have done it myself, or tried to, but dammit, Angela, you live here. I couldn't just drop everything and come flying out to Caley Cove on a whim.'

'Maybe you couldn't.' She wiped a trickle of moisture off her forehead. 'You could, on the other hand, have *asked* me to do my best with Charlotte, instead of phoning up and snapping out orders like the lord of the manor dispatching a handy scullery maid to mop up an unpleasant spill. I've never heard such codswallop in my life.'

Ryan's eyebrows shot up alarmingly. 'Codswallop? Are you calling the possibility of being engaged to me *codswallop?*'

Angela wasn't sure, but she thought he was having trouble suppressing a smile. 'That's what it is, isn't it?' she replied reasonably, but with a dull slumping of the heart. 'You don't in the least want to marry me.'

'No,' he agreed, stepping beneath the shade of a vine maple that was growing just outside the fence. 'I don't. But I'm not altogether opposed to other, less permanent arrangements ... ' His voice trailed off and his eyes sent a hotly explicit message.

Oh. So that was what this was all about. Ryan had been mulling over his options and decided she'd do after all. Which was what she'd wanted. Wasn't it? So why, in all this heat, did she feel cold?

'Are you going to open this gate and let me in?' Ryan asked conversationally as the sun cast changing shadows across his face.

Angela rested her foot on the shovel

and wiped a damp arm across her eyes. When she lowered it, he was still there, leaning against the tree-trunk with his arms crossed. She couldn't tell what he was thinking, but there was a tension about him now that made her think he might not be as relaxed as he sounded.

She thought about telling him that no, she had no intention of letting him in. But just at that moment he moved, and her gaze was drawn irresistibly downwards as his unbuttoned white shirt fell away to reveal a hard expanse of chest and taut midriff. Brief denim shorts served only to cover the bare essentials, and when her eyes dropped to his thighs she remembered with a devastating surge of body heat just how those thighs had felt pressed against hers on the dance-floor . . . and when he had kissed her . . .

Without quite meaning to, she allowed the shovel to drop from her hands.

It wasn't until she had the gate open, and saw him glance at her with faint mockery as he passed, that she remembered she was wearing dirty khaki shorts, a torn yellow vest-top and a great deal of perspiration. Hardly the correct attire for an engagement.

Which was just as well, she reminded herself as his bronzed arm brushed against her dusty one. Because there wasn't going to be any engagement.

'I haven't heard from Charlotte,' she said abruptly, because she was appallingly conscious of his closeness and felt she had to say something. 'Nor have I heard that she's feeling fragile.'

'She isn't,' Ryan replied calmly, ignoring the dust and taking hold of her arm. He led her across to the patio. 'I phoned her back a few minutes after you hung up on me.'

'Oh?' Angela stared at him suspiciously, and saw that he was wearing that familiarly maddening little smile.

'Mm. I told her we'd have news for her this weekend.'

'News? You didn't . . . ?'

'No. I made no promises. Just told

her not to count on anything, and that she mustn't bother you in case it upset my future plans.'

Angela's hand flew to her mouth. 'You didn't! Oh, poor Charlotte.'

'Poor Charlotte? I owe my aunt a lot, but don't you think your sympathy's misdirected?'

'Not altogether. It must have driven her crazy, not being able to pump me for explanations.'

Ryan laughed, and she saw that the tension she had noted earlier was gone. 'I'm sure it did. Now, Ms Baddingley, how about you go and wash off all that dirt, and slip into something equally revealing but more appetising — ?'

'I don't want to be eaten,' said Angela, quickly but not quite truthfully. She wouldn't at all mind his mouth on . . . She gulped.

'And I'll finish digging that flowerbed for you,' he finished, ignoring the interruption. 'We'll consider our respective appetites when I'm through.'

Appetites . . . Angela swallowed again

and tried not to concentrate on the faint damp sheen of his skin and that sexy smile, and . . .

He put a hand on her shoulder and turned her pointedly around. 'Go on,' he said.

As Angela gave up and stumbled into the house, she wondered if she had really felt that intimate little pat on a part of her that nobody had taken the liberty of patting for some time.

She stood in the shower and let the cool water wash away the heat and dust along with any inclination to think beyond the next half-hour. There was no point in thinking. Ryan had come back. To solve a problem for himself, not for her. But it didn't seem to make any difference. All that mattered was that he was here.

Ten minutes later, dressed in her most demure blue sundress, she went back out to the garden.

Ryan's back was to her. He had thrown off his shirt, and, having just finished digging the flowerbed, was leaning on the shovel with one foot resting on the blade. Angela stood still, lost in bemused admiration of the tough, bronzed skin stretched across the muscles of his shoulders, the thick, bright head of hair and the endless legs sheathed in fine gold.

Dear heaven, he was a beautiful man.

After a while he seemed to sense her watching him, because he turned slowly, gave her a lazy smile and held out his arms.

Angela ran her tongue over lips that had suddenly gone dry. He'd been deliciously enticing from the back. From the front he was overwhelming. Sweat beaded on the skin of a broad chest and flat abdomen on which there wasn't an ounce of extra fat. His head was thrown back to expose the strong column of his throat, and with the sun beating down on him he looked like a golden god of the afternoon. Vaguely, Angela remembered another time he'd reminded her of a god. But just then he moved and she was left in no doubt that he was mortal. Mouth-wateringly, achingly mortal.

He was walking towards her, still with his arms outstretched, but the smile on his lips was no longer lazy.

Angela attempted to turn away and found she couldn't. He stopped about ten inches in front of her.

'I . . . ' She tried to speak, but only managed a whisper. 'Ryan, you said it wouldn't work. Why — ?'

'Because I'm a mortal man,' he replied, echoing her thoughts of a few moments before. 'And I want you more than I've ever wanted a woman in my life. I'm afraid, Angela, darling, that the moment you hung up that phone I knew I'd made a mistake. So I handled Aunt Charlotte in the swiftest way I could think of, pressed Martin into helping with my caseload — and now I'm here to make you pay the price.'

Her eyes widened. 'What price?'

'The price for hanging up on me, of course.' His tone was light, but his mouth and his eyes told her he meant business.

Angela stepped back. Some instinct of survival convinced her that she should. But the sea was pounding the rocks at the bottom of the cliff, a plane was droning overhead, and her senses were drowning in the hot, blatant scent of his desire.

Even so, she tried. 'Ryan, I don't think — '

He stepped forward and scooped her up in his arms. 'Where?' he asked. 'Bed? Or right here among the buttercups and daisies?'

'Someone might see,' she gasped, not taking in at once that her words implied eager consent.

'Right. Bed,' he said decisively, and Angela locked her arms around his neck as he strode with her into the house, marched across the living-room and looked around for the door to her bedroom.

When he didn't find it at once he put her down, so that she was half standing, half sitting against her small maple table with space for four.

Ryan watched her struggle for breath, his eyes dark now and smoky with passion. Then his hands closed over her hips, slid down her thighs, and she felt the blue dress bunch up at her waist. After that his thumbs were inside the waistband of her panties, slipping them down until a faint breeze began to tease her skin. She gasped, and clung to his shoulders as he bent his head and buried his face in her neck. She felt his lips move to the hollow of her throat, then down further to the smooth cleavage of her breasts. As her fingers raked across his back, the two of them sank together on to the carpet, and the dress Angela had put on only minutes earlier was hauled over her head and tossed into a heap beneath the table.

Ryan propped himself up on one elbow and his smoky gaze wandered almost reverently over the damp, soft skin of her body, fresh from the shower.

'You're beautiful, my angel,' he

murmured, stroking her hair. 'The most beautiful angel I've ever seen.'

Then he lowered his mouth over hers, and Angela moved her hands to his waist to unclasp the button of his shorts. He wasn't wearing a belt, and a second later they joined her discarded dress on the floor.

His fingers parted her thighs with gentle insistence, and as the rapture of his touch inflamed her with undreamed-of pleasure Angela cried out, 'Ryan, I love you!'

The heat of the day merged with the heat in their bodies, so that when they came together it was with an explosion of shared ecstasy that for a little while blotted out the sun.

Some time later, Angela shifted her back on the sturdy beige carpet, turned to Ryan who was lying beside her, and said with a not-quite-steady laugh, 'I guess we didn't make it to the bed.'

'No.' He didn't look at her, went on staring at the ceiling.

She studied the hardness around his

mouth and jawline, took in the fists closed tightly at his sides, and said quietly, 'It's all right. You needn't worry. I just said it in the heat of the moment.'

'Some heat,' murmured Ryan, his tone unusually husky. 'Some moment.' He didn't look at her, but he touched a hand to her cheek.

They were silent for a while, then Angela turned on her side, discovered the floor was becoming uncomfortably hard, and sat up. When she looked down at Ryan, she saw that his mind had flown to some dark place where she couldn't follow.

'I said it's all right,' she repeated.

'I know. I'm glad.' Briefly his eyes met hers, but they were empty, as if he was a long way away.

Angela frowned and scrabbled under the table for her dress. She pulled it over her head and tossed Ryan his shorts. He ignored them.

'What's eating you?' she demanded with sudden bitterness. 'You got what you came for, didn't you?'

'What I came for?' The look he gave her was as bleak as a mountaintop in winter. 'Yes, I suppose I did.'

'And was it satisfactory?' She didn't mean to be sarcastic, but she knew her mouth was twisted in a sneer.

Ryan's arm shot up to grab her wrist, and before she realised what was happening he had pulled her down so that their faces were very nearly touching. 'Incredibly satisfactory,' he growled, not looking bleak any more. 'But that wasn't the only reason I came back.' He stroked his free hand gently over her bottom, and she gave a little groan and collapsed on top of him.

'What were the other reasons?' she whispered, curling her fingers in his hair.

'Aunt Charlotte for one.' He was still stroking.

Angela squirmed at his touch. 'Making passionate love to me on my carpet isn't likely to convince Charlotte there's no hope,' she muttered into his neck.

'True.' He patted her soft flesh

absently. 'But that wasn't part of my original plan. I meant to chastise you for your telephone manners, of course, take you to bed, not the carpet, and after that — '

'After that, what?' asked Angela, almost certain she didn't want to hear his answer, but unable to stop herself from asking.

He ran his thumb slowly up her spine, and took his time about answering. When he did, there was an odd note of discord in his voice. 'I'm not at all sure. Take you to bed again, I suppose.'

'That's no answer,' murmured Angela. Whatever she'd expected him to say, it certainly hadn't been that. Puzzled, she closed her eyes for a moment. Then Ryan shifted beneath her and heat began to flare up in her loins.

'Oh, yes, it is an answer,' he replied, with such unexpected harshness that immediately her body went rigid. 'As long as you continue to see me as no more than an afternoon's fun in the sun, you and I will be fine together, Angel. But often when people start something they don't know how to stop. And I don't mean that to happen to us.'

'Why should it happen?' Her voice was muffled by his shoulder as the heat inside her died down to a smouldering ember and a twisting pain settled deep in her gut. What she wanted to say was, Why should we stop?

'It won't, I promise you.' Abruptly he rolled her off him on to the floor. 'I learned long ago to rely on no one but myself — not to need anything from anyone. It's a lesson you'd do well to learn too. Don't ever depend on me, Angel. Others have, and they've lived to regret it.'

Angela heard Al, who was sleeping on top of his cage, flap his stunted wings and natter softly, and she pushed herself up on one arm to look down into the face of this strong, utterly self-contained man whose own wings had once been cruelly clipped. His eyes were mirror-flat and mysterious. He was smiling that full, sensuous smile she had come to love, but which she had always recognised was touched with its own brand of bitterness. How could she possibly know what he'd been through? How much hurt was he walling off inside? Only his surface scars had ever been permitted to show.

Absently she ran her thumb along the white line above his eye as she tried to form a response that wouldn't betray her love and — not dependence but *need* to a man who looked on freedom from the bonds of love as a way of life. It would serve no purpose to let him know that she loved him, because he had spoken the truth when he said she'd live to regret it. As she had, in the end, regretted her commitment to Kelvin. She couldn't make the same mistake again. And Ryan might not want to hurt her — she was fairly sure he didn't — but she suspected that any knowledge of her desperate vulnerability would only serve to hasten his departure. And in the process she would lose her pride as well.

'Ryan,' she began slowly, 'don't you think . . . ?' She stopped. What was that noise outside the window? It sounded like something tapping against the glass. Was the patio door still open? She had an uncomfortable feeling it was. Of course the table was in an L-shaped alcove, so they shouldn't be visible from outside, but . . .

'Put your shorts on,' she hissed at Ryan. 'Now.'

She saw his eyebrows go up, and she thought he was about to tell her he'd get dressed when he damned well chose to. But he must have read the urgency in her eyes, because without a word he picked up the shorts and pulled them on at the same time as she reached behind his head for her panties.

They were still in her hand when she heard the soft slap of shoes against the carpet. A few seconds later a shock of white hair appeared around the wall of the L.

'Angela? You left your door open, and I saw the car, so — '

The gruff voice broke off abruptly as sharp eyes took in the tableau on the floor. 'Good God. What the . . . ?' Ryan's father cleared his throat for several seconds. 'Harrumph. Angela, my dear . . . just came to return those books you loaned me. Didn't expect . . . ' He shook his head groggily, then turned to face his son. 'I mean, it's no good your . . . ' He cleared his throat again. 'Never occurred to me I'd find — '

'It's all right, Harry, you didn't — ' This time it was Angela's turn to break off. She had been about to assure Ryan's father that he hadn't interrupted anything, but she realised in time that that would only make things worse.

Ryan came to the rescue. 'Hi, Dad,' he said, coolly fastening the button on his shorts. 'Didn't mean to startle you. I've just been helping Angela find her contacts.'

As Angela scrambled to her feet she squashed her panties into a ball and shoved them awkwardly into the pocket of her dress. There wasn't a hope in hell that Harry would believe Ryan's unlikely story about her contacts, but at least it would enable them all to save face.

Ryan rose with his customary grace and made his way into Angela's kitchen as if he owned it. 'Tea, Dad?' he suggested over his shoulder. 'I'm sure we could all do with a cup.'

9

'That was quick thinking.' Angela was still red-faced and breathless when she joined Ryan in the kitchen after settling Harry on the sofa with a pile of magazines and a book called *Gardening Your Excess Body Fat Away*.

'Thinking on one's feet — or in this case flat on one's back — is a talent acquired swiftly behind bars.' Ryan didn't look at her as he helped himself to a teapot and three china mugs. Angela bent over to slip her panties on, and he added, 'So is protecting one's rear,' as he patted her smartly on hers.

She straightened indignantly, already flustered, and annoyed by his flippant self-possession. 'How can you think about tea at a time like this?' she demanded.

'I'm Charlotte Koniski's nephew,' he

replied, as if that left no more to be said.

'Yes, but your father — '

'Dad enjoys a good cup of tea.'

'That's not what I meant, and you know it.' Angela resented the fact that Ryan was well in control of a situation that had her temporarily unhinged.

'Look,' he said, taking her by the shoulders and transfixing her with an austere grey eye, 'there is nothing to be gained by acting as if we've committed a crime, when all we've actually done is spend a very pleasant hour on a private carpet. *Your* carpet. As far as my father is concerned, as long as the proprieties have been observed on the surface — '

'But they haven't been. He *knows*.' Angela, remembering the expression on Harry's face, was still distraught.

'Of course he does. Don't worry about it, I'll handle Dad.'

'Yes, but how? I mean — '

'Angel, stop quivering like a sacrificial virgin — which I have reason to know you are not — and go pour tea for my father. You can discuss the weather with him — or the mountains, his health, or anything else you can think of that doesn't involve a detailed explanation of our activities on your dining-room floor.'

'I doubt if they need an explanation. And I am not quivering.' Angela began arranging mugs on a tray and loading sugar lumps into the milk jug.

'Aren't you? Then you won't have any trouble pouring tea.' Ryan hitched a hip on the edge of the table and folded his arms as if he were laying claim to her kitchen.

Seeing the small, amused smile on his face, Angela suspected he thought she was so disconcerted by Harry's unexpected arrival that she'd drop the teapot. It was exactly the spur she needed to take herself in hand and stop worrying about Harry's sensibilities. If his son wasn't concerned, why should she be?

Lifting her chin, she picked up the tray and marched back into the living-room, where she found Harry pretending to study a picture of a middle-aged man planting potatoes. Ryan, his shirt hanging loosely over his shorts, sauntered in behind her and stretched himself in a wicker chair that seemed too small for him.

Harry put down the potato-planter and turned to glower at his son. Angela noted that his hands were trembling, and that he seemed older than he had a week ago.

No, she thought. Oh, no! Please don't let him have another attack because of me. She glanced at Ryan, lounging in his chair, and saw that although he looked at ease his eyes had narrowed.

She was opening her mouth to say something — anything — that would bring the colour back to Harry's cheeks, when Ryan announced with a smile that looked quite natural and unforced, 'Well, Dad, as I expect you've already figured out, Angela and I have just become engaged. You're the first to know.' Not waiting for Harry's relieved congratulations, or his alleged fiancée's strangled gasp of protest, he expanded the smile and directed it with bland implacability at Angela. 'Haven't we, my angel?'

Angela clutched at the arms of the hard tapestry chair she was sitting on and discovered it didn't have any arms. 'What did you say?' she asked, gripping her fingers together in her lap and wondering if her face had turned purple.

'I said we'd just become engaged.' The look he gave her told her as words couldn't have that if she tried to deny it she was likely to find herself in worse trouble than an unwanted engagement. As if Harry's imminent collapse weren't bad enough!

For a moment she attempted to tell herself that she was a mature woman who'd been running her own law firm for years. And that Ryan had no right to run her life. Then she looked at Harry, his craggy face creased with delight, and the words she had been about to speak froze on her lips. Her disbelieving gaze switched to Ryan, and she remembered how that lean body had felt moving over hers as she'd held him ecstatically in her arms — and she knew that in spite of all her sensible resolutions if he asked her to marry him tomorrow, in all seriousness, no power on earth could make her refuse. She would think about that revelation later. In the meantime, he'd got them into this farce and it was up to him to get them out.

'Er — yes,' she mumbled, turning back to Harry, and giving him a brilliant, empty smile. 'We — we haven't set a date, of course . . . ' Her voice trailed off.

'Course not. Haven't had time yet, have you?' Harry's bright eyes flicked from Angela's flustered face to Ryan's composed one. 'Hmm. All very sudden,' he said gruffly. 'Still, have to admit I'm glad to hear it. Only thing to do, considering . . . Hmm.' He strummed the fingers of one hand against his knee. 'Know your aunt will be pleased. Think she's been counting on it.'

'Mm.' Ryan stretched his arms lazily over his head. 'She told me it was time I did my duty as a son and made an effort to carry on the Koniski line. I promised to work on it.' He gave his father a broad and not remotely guilty grin.

Harry said, 'Harrumph,' tried hard not to return the grin, and failed.

Al said, 'Grack,' from his corner, and for a moment Angela wished she could consign all three of them to a place long rumoured to be hotter than Caley Cove.

Harry left soon after, with a muttered warning to his son to behave himself in a manner befitting Angela's betrothed.

As Ryan stood in the doorway with his arm around her waist, he remarked that it was too bad his father hadn't heeded Dr Colombo's warning not to drive yet.

'What, and have him miss the chance

232

to broadcast the scoop of the year?' said Angela with unintended bitterness. She took a deep breath and stared straight ahead at the gate. 'OK, party's over, Ryan. Now tell me what that was all about.'

'Damage control,' he replied promptly, turning her round, spinning her into the house and marching her into the living-room. 'Dad looked ready to collapse from the shock of catching us in what I believe used to be called a compromising position. And you, Ms Baddingley, have a reputation to maintain in this town.'

'And you haven't?'

'Of course not. I, my angel, am well beyond redemption.' He spoke lightly but with an underlying grimness. 'You're not. If I hadn't told Dad we were engaged, the moment he got home he'd have told Aunt Charlotte what he'd seen — in strictest confidence, of course. And sooner or later she'd have told Mrs Bracken — in confidence. Mrs Bracken would have told Mrs Gruber, who would have told Mrs Farraday, who would have told Mrs Malone, and soon the entire communication network would have heard that Caley Cove's respectable lady lawyer was a fallen woman.'

'I only fell as far as the carpet,' said Angela with consummate irrelevance.

Ryan made a choking sound that reminded her of the frogs that croaked all summer in Mackenzie's Pond. 'Far enough,' he muttered. 'The point, though, is that as long as we're engaged your reputation will remain tarnished but intact.'

'But we're not engaged,' Angela protested, pushing his arm away and wandering over to inspect a sleepy Al. 'Or did I miss something? You didn't propose to me while I was pouring tea, did you? Or while the two of us were — um — otherwise engaged on the carpet?'

'Not that I know of. Would you have accepted me if I had?' He came up behind her and wrapped his arms around her ribcage. She could feel him all along the length of her back.

'No,' lied Angela at once. 'Of course not.'

Before she had time to compose her features, he had turned her around and was staring down into her face.

After a while she saw the corner of his lip curl up. 'Not flattering, but I suppose it simplifies matters,' he said with a shrug.

Angela, unable to bear this amused remoteness after the passion they had shared such a short time before, twisted away from him and said tightly, 'There's a phone in the kitchen. You'd better get on it at once.'

'To spread the news of our engagement? Dad will handle that more than efficiently.'

'No. To tell your father and, I suppose your aunt, that it isn't true.'

'I'm not telling them anything of the sort.'

'But you must. Ryan, this may be an amusing game to you — '

'I don't play games. Life's too short.'

'Stop it!' she cried, only just managing not to stamp her foot. 'Of course you're playing games. We're not engaged and we never will be. You don't want to marry me any more than I want to marry you.'

'No,' agreed Ryan. 'I don't.' He raised his eyes and stared at a point above her head. 'But it may surprise you to know that there was a time, not long after I was released, when I considered marriage. That was how I learned that men like me are better off walking alone. In the long run it saves grief all round — '

'Then what's all this nonsense about an engagement?' Angela found she didn't want to stamp her foot any more. Ridiculously, she wanted to cry. But she wasn't going to. Not now, and not later either.

'It's not nonsense, my angel. You and I are now officially engaged.'

'Oh, no, we're not,' said Angela. 'I don't get engaged to men I'm not going to marry.'

'All right, then. If you insist, we'll get married.'

'I don't insist — '

'No, but I do. At least on the engagement. And since you're obviously not anxious to spend your life clinging to me like some dewy-eyed little homebody, I suppose there's no reason we shouldn't make it legal. Afterwards we can go on leading our separate lives.'

'Oh,' jeered Angela, now desperately confused and wondering if he really meant to break her heart. 'You mean a classic marriage of inconvenience. No, thank you, I wouldn't want you to put yourself out. Incidentally, what on earth makes you think I'd be interested?'

He lifted an eyebrow. 'I'd have thought that was obvious.'

'Oh, I see.' She walked across to the window, stared at the buttercups, then came back and thumped herself down on the sofa. 'Yes, you have a very nice body, Mr Koniski. I quite enjoyed it. But, frankly, it falls short of inspiring me to marriage.'

Ryan's eyes narrowed. 'You want inspiration, Ms Baddingley?' he asked silkily. 'I believe I can supply it.' He sat down beside her and ran his hand purposefully up the inside of her leg. When he heard her gasp, he added as if he were discussing faulty plumbing, 'In fact, though, I was talking about the need to maintain your reputation in this town.'

Angela drew back, stared disbelievingly into his face. He looked sober, as controlled as ever, and maybe even a little bored.

'Are you out of your mind?' she demanded. 'You're suggesting I should marry you because your father caught us cavorting on the carpet?'

'That too. Can you think of a better reason?'

'Yes. Several. Liking, friendship, companionship. I've even heard of people marrying for love. But in this day and age I haven't heard of a woman getting married because someone might get the idea that at the age of thirty-five she's not actually living the life of a nun.'

'But you have been more or less, haven't you?' He removed his hand from her leg, and she let out her breath.

Angela frowned. 'That's not the point.'

'No. The point is that even in this day and age you happen to be living in Caley Cove. Believe me, I've had first-hand experience of what gossip can do to a person's reputation in this town. I'd sooner spare you that but, frankly, at this stage my main concern is for my father.'

'He did look a bit — white.'

'Exactly. He's endured enough pain because of me. Now his health is precarious, and I'm not about to subject him to further distress. He'll accept what he saw quite happily just so long as you and I are planning to marry. What would upset him beyond belief is the knowledge that I took advantage of your innocence — little he knows! — with no plans to make you an honest woman. That, my sweet angel, is why we are staying engaged.'

'But that's not fair. He's *your* father — '

'And your friend. Do you really want to be responsible for his having another attack?'

'Ryan, that's blackmail.'

'Call it what you like. The fact is, I won't have my father upset. And as for your reputation, if you deny our engagement this soon after it's announced — and believe me it has been announced, I know my father — you'll soon find out what gossip can do to you around here. People will stop talking the moment you enter a room, and start up again the moment you leave.' He pulled up the strap of her sundress which had fallen down over one shoulder. 'And you'll begin to feel as if you're living in a fish bowl with black olive all over your teeth.'

Angela heard the note of resigned bitterness in his voice and wasn't surprised. He'd suffered from the wagging tongues of this town. 'I don't think fish eat black olives,' she muttered, feeling out of her depth, miserable, and altogether too warm. 'Anyway it's not me you're concerned about, it's your father.'

'I'm concerned about both of you. Dad principally, yes.' He smiled disarmingly, and picked up a strand of her hair, making Angela wish he wouldn't sit so close. 'And now that we have that settled . . . '

'Ryan!' she exclaimed, moving as far away from him as she could. 'We are *not* getting married. And if you . . . '

Ryan stood up and strolled out of the room as if she hadn't spoken.

Angela sank back against the cushions and fixed her gaze blankly on the hard bright blue of the sky. A minute later Ryan strolled back in looking complacent.

'All taken care of,' he said, crossing his arms and leaning against the mantel with an incendiary glint in his eye. 'I've just confirmed everything with Aunt Charlotte and Dad. They're talking about a September wedding — '

'Ryan . . . ' Angela stood up, and began to advance on him with her fists pressed tight against her sides. 'I am not marrying you in September — '

'August, then.'

'Or any other month — '

'Fine. We'll have a long engagement.'

'We will not have any kind of engagement.'

'Oh, yes, we will.' He smiled his implacable, heart-stopping smile, and just for a moment Angela wished she could give in, wished hopelessly that circumstances were different and that Ryan loved her. She didn't care what he'd done in the past. He was obviously a man with honourable instincts, or he wouldn't care so much about the father who had once let him down. And he certainly wouldn't consider her reputation.

She stopped wanting to give in when he continued calmly, 'Don't waste time arguing with me, Angela. You want my liking, companionship, friendship? You have them. As for love . . . ' He paused, and the lines around his eyes seemed to deepen. 'As for love, that's a luxury I've never been able to afford.' He took a step towards her as she stood glaring up at him with the light of battle glittering in her eye. 'And if the expression on your lovely face is anything to go by, I think I can safely assume you feel the same way I do. We ought to get along very well.'

'We are not going to get along at all,' shouted Angela. She had to shout. Somehow the noise helped to blot out a blast of unexpected pain. 'Don't you understand? I don't *want* to get married. Or engaged. I just want to carry on with my life the way it was before you turned up to disrupt it.'

'You won't be able to.' He sounded genuinely sorry and a little irritated. 'Caley Cove won't let you. And if that doesn't matter to you, *I* won't let you. Maybe in a few months, when Dad's condition is more stable, we can break it to him and Aunt Charlotte that things aren't working out between us. For now, we will make tentative wedding plans for next year, and put as good a face on the situation as we can.'

'And if I refuse?'

He closed the space between them and put his hands on her waist. 'But you won't refuse, will you?' His pewter eyes were clear and unswerving. 'Because you'd never be able to live with yourself if anything happened to my father.'

Angela forced herself to look away from those impossible eyes. It might be sheer blackmail, but his persistence was beginning to wear her down. And he was right, of course. She wouldn't hurt Harry for the world.

Ryan must have seen that she was wavering, because he said briskly, 'Good. That's that, then.' When Angela opened her mouth to contradict him, he growled, 'Shut up, for a heaven's sake,' and closed it firmly with a kiss.

Angela, with Al once again perched on her shoulder, sat in the dark on her patio, gazing out at the blackness over the water. It was cooler now, and a faint breeze stroked the surface of her skin. Somewhere in the night she could smell honeysuckle. She was still trying to figure out what had hit her.

Two hours ago Ryan had left her to return to Seattle. And somehow, in the early hours of the evening, she seemed to have got herself engaged. With no particular effort, and without actually appearing to be a one-man tank formation, Ryan Koniski had reorganised her life.

She supposed she ought to feel happy because, without quite knowing how it had come about, she had agreed to become engaged to the man she loved. She had also, and totally against her better judgement, consented to make vague wedding plans for next year. Not that she really believed Ryan meant to marry her, of course, in spite of his casual reference to separate lives. Yet he had seemed sincere, and willing to marry provided it didn't interfere with the way he lived — apart, she supposed, from the occasional conjugal visit to Caley Cove in order to keep his family and the grapevine on low frequency.

Angela closed her eyes, shutting out the night. How had she got herself into this mess? She, who ever since Kelvin's betrayal had been as opposed to commitment as Ryan was, had intended to remain forever single. She had even, and with only a half-formed regret, given up her youthful dream of having babies. Her sister's two children had at least partially filled that empty space in her life. When she saw them. Which wasn't often enough.

She sighed, thinking how quickly everything had changed. Now she wanted to commit herself to Ryan, who didn't love her. To bear his children at the ripe old age of thirty-five. And indeed she *was* committed. To what she wasn't even sure. Whatever it was, she knew that in the end it would tear her apart.

So why had she given in to his single-minded blackmail?

'I'm a fool, Al,' she murmured with a sigh. 'A full-time, overgrown buffoon.'

'Grack,' chirped Al agreeably, poking his beak at her ear.

Two Saturdays later, Angela stood in front of her wardrobe and once again called herself a fool. Ryan's boot case was due to start on Monday, but last night he had phoned to say there was nothing more he could do before the trial, so he was taking time out to visit his fiancée.

'The tongues will start to wag if I don't,' he had explained acidly.

Angela hadn't bothered to tell him that the tongues were already wagging. As Ryan had predicted, Harry had told Charlotte what he'd seen, and inevitably the news had spread from there. But, also as he'd predicted, their engagement had nipped the worst of the gossip in the bud, and several of the town's matrons had actually told her they would be happier doing business with a married woman — even if Ryan Koniski was the husband.

'Charlotte thinks marriage will settle him,' Mavis Bracken had explained, nodding sagely.

Angela wished she could settle Mavis Bracken's busy mouth.

Now, as she stood gazing into her wardrobe, it occurred to her that this was the first time she had actually known ahead of time that Ryan was about to erupt into her life. Every other time they'd met, he had just appeared.

She pulled out a mauve print sundress, decided against it, and was about to put it back when she heard a car pulling into the driveway. Ryan was early. Damn. Once again he'd taken her by surprise.

Tugging a soiled cotton T-shirt over her head, she slipped her shorts off and reached for the mauve dress. It would have to do.

'No need to do that,' drawled a silky smooth voice from the doorway. 'You're already slightly overdressed.'

Angela started and whirled irritably around. 'How did you get in?' she demanded.

'Through the door. With the spare key I borrowed two weeks ago.'

'I didn't give you a spare key.'

'I know. Very remiss of you. That's why I took it. And why are you putting on that mauve thing when I specifically told you not to?' He flung himself down on her bed and held out a hand. 'Come here. Let's get the rest of those clothes off.'

'Is that all you came for?' asked Angela, dropping the dress and fidgeting with the strap of her bra.

'All? You call that *all*? I thought it was a very moving experience.'

'It was moving all right,' she muttered. 'Ryan, I don't think we should — '

He propped himself up on one elbow and leaned over the edge of the bed to grab her hand. 'Of course we should,' he said firmly. 'We're engaged. Remember?' He gave her arm a sharp tug and she collapsed on to the bed beside him.

Angela remembered. 'Don't,' she groaned. He was wearing the loose white shirt again, this time over fawn-coloured trousers, and the hard expanse of his chest as he pulled her to him was sending delicious memories steaming to her brain.

'Why not?' he murmured, inserting the tip of his tongue in her ear, so that for a moment she was reminded of Al.

'Because . . . ' With painful determination, she ignored the steaming memories, struggled to a sitting position and pulled her hands out of his grasp. 'Because — I don't know, I suppose because it makes me feel used.'

Ryan's warm smile turned cold in front of her eyes. 'I see. Is that what you think? But you, of course, weren't using me?'

'I don't know.' She stumbled to her feet, picked up the mauve dress and dragged it over her head. 'Maybe I was.'

'Great.' Ryan shifted his shoulders against the bedspread, but made no effort to rise. 'So it was a case of mutual opportunism, was it? Well, that seems safely uninvolving.' He swung his legs abruptly to the floor. 'All right, grab your purse. I'm taking you out.'

'Out? But why — ?'

'Because if I don't I'm liable to do something old-fashioned and unpardonably chauvinistic. You are beginning to get my goat, Ms Angela Baddingley.'

Angela eyed first the lines of frustration around his mouth and then the large hands clasped loosely between his knees. She decided not to ask for clarification.

'There's no need to make like the school bully,' she said loftily. 'You're not at all convincing in the part.' He was, but it wouldn't do him any good to know it. 'Where are we going?'

'Lake Crescent. We'll have lunch at the hotel. After that we will go for a long, strenuous walk that should serve the same purpose as a cold shower.

Then I'll take you round to visit Dad and Aunt Charlotte. She's dying to discuss trousseaus — or whatever it is women find to discuss about weddings.'

He sounded so dour and disgruntled that Angela felt a brief twinge of guilt. He was, after all, willing to marry her, which must mean he cared something for her feelings. If he was serious. Then she remembered that the engagement was his idea, that he had practically blackmailed her into it, and that her reasons for giving in to him were so complicated that she hadn't yet figured them out herself. Surely she was confused enough as it was without complicating the issue any further. And her reaction to Ryan's touch, even to a glance from his hooded grey eyes, was definitely a complication.

They drove to Lake Crescent with the car top down, and more or less in silence. Angela enjoyed watching the wind whip through his hair, making him look young and carefree as he rarely did until he smiled. She enjoyed his sure touch on the wheel, the feeling of speed and power, and the rush of air past her face. By the time they arrived at the secluded, log-cabin-style hotel set amid the trees beside the lake, she was relaxed, and ready to regard Ryan without suspicion — at least temporarily — as the attractive but complex man she had fallen in love with.

He, on the other hand, now that they had stopped, looked as if was ready to take on an army for the sheer pleasure of drawing lots of blood. Angela wondered if she was the army.

She allowed him to lead her into the hotel's log-beamed entrance hall, and somehow she wasn't surprised that they were shown to the best table by the dining-room window even though they were wearing casual clothes. Ryan wasn't the sort of man you seated next to the service entrance, and it showed whether or not he dressed the part.

Vaguely, Angela remembered Sarah telling her that she had come here with Brett not long after they met. If only her relationship with Ryan could have a happy ending . . .

'Beautiful view,' she said, for the sake of saying something, and latching without effort on to the one obviously safe topic. Besides, it *was* beautiful out there with the inevitable sun turning the centre of the lake to a sheet of gold, and the green fronds of the evergreens reflected in the darker waters near the shore. There were small white butterflies fluttering in the light outside the window.

Ryan nodded non-committally and turned to order champagne from the white-coated waiter.

'Champagne?' said Angela. 'For lunch?'

'Not done in Caley Cove?' he asked with an edge to his voice.

'Not done by Angela Baddingley. It puts me to sleep.'

'Not today it won't. You won't get the chance. And we're having champagne to celebrate our engagement.'

'Ryan, seriously.' Angela made a desperate attempt to set things straight.

'The more I think about it, the more I'm sure that we shouldn't go through with this farce. I mean, I do like you, and I guess you must like me a bit or you wouldn't have proposed — well, sort of proposed — but I must have been insane to go along with such a crazy idea. You don't want a wife, I don't want a husband — '

'OK,' said Ryan. 'Suit yourself.' He picked up a roll and began to butter it just as the waiter came back with the champagne.

Angela had a feeling all the colour had drained out of her face. 'What did you say?' she asked.

'I said suit yourself.' He lifted his glass, studied the spiralling gold bubbles, tasted, and nodded at the waiter. Then, without asking Angela what she wanted, he ordered artichoke hearts and salmon steaks for them both.

Angela didn't care what she ate, and wasn't sure she'd manage to eat at all. She hadn't expected Ryan to capitulate so easily, and now she was forced to acknowledge that she wasn't entirely sure she had wanted him to cancel their pseudo-engagement. In fact she had been acting like a scared little girl. She loved Ryan, but he didn't love her, and because she couldn't make up her mind what she ought to do she had let him make it up for her. And today she had been looking for reassurance. She hadn't got it. Instead the ball had been tossed right out of court.

'Because I wouldn't let you make love to me?' she asked, thinking that the lake didn't look nearly as beautiful any more.

Ryan put down his glass. 'Are you asking me if I told you to suit yourself because you wouldn't fall into my bed?' He spoke conversationally, but she thought she detected an icy frustration beneath the calm. And how could she blame him? She wasn't making a whole lot of sense.

'It was my bed actually,' she muttered, with a vague sense that she'd had this conversation once before. When he gave her the sort of look she suspected he usually reserved for his more dedicated delinquents, she added honestly, 'I don't know. I guess I'm just not used to feeling this confused.'

'Look,' he said, his features softening marginally, 'we both know it's the most sensible solution. Apart from the fact that it should prevent my father from having a relapse and Aunt Charlotte from going into a decline, it will also allow you to go on living happily in this town.'

'And what will you get out of it?' asked Angela. 'A bedmate?'

His lips tightened, and remained grimly pressed together as the waiter set their plates down in front of them. But when they were alone again he replied evenly, 'If this morning was anything to go by, I doubt if I can count on that, can I? Is the idea so repulsive to you, Angela? If it is, you're a better actress than I thought.'

Angela looked up from her salmon. There was something in his voice, something raw and unusually exposed, that made her wonder if he was as emotionally detached as she'd imagined. But his face, closed and enigmatic as ever, gave no clue.

'Does it matter?' she asked, frowning.

Exasperation flickered in his eyes and was gone. 'I'm not a monster, Angela. I don't take that which isn't freely given.'

'You offered me your hand in marriage. It's not unreasonable to expect something in return.'

This time it was more than a flicker, it was a flash of steel. 'If you knew me better, you'd know I don't go in for bribery to get what I want.'

No, just blackmail, thought Angela. But she didn't say it, because beneath the hard rasp of his words she was almost sure she heard — no, surely not pain?

Had she hurt him? She hadn't meant to, hadn't thought she could. And she wanted to put her arms around him right here in front of the window of this busy dining-room with the large-bosomed lady in red at the next table looking on. Instead she said quietly, 'It's true I don't know you. Ryan — you don't want me to love you? Do you?'

He put his knife down so abruptly that it clanged against the side of his plate, and, before he turned away to glare out over the lake, just for a moment he allowed his guard to drop — and she thought she caught a glimpse of the lonely, tortured man beneath the mask.

'No,' he said, so harshly that she winced. 'I don't. Why would I want to inflict that miserable affliction on you? I suggested our engagement as a convenient and *safe* solution to a problem. There is no safety in love.' He wrenched his gaze from the window and turned to face her, and when he spoke again his voice was hoarse. 'You don't, do you? Love me?'

Angela stared at the set, stony face with the bleak eyes, and she fought to beat back the tears he mustn't see. She was a truthful woman; it hurt her to answer the most important question of her life with a lie. But she knew that if she told the truth now Ryan would get up and leave her where she sat, with a plate full of half-eaten salmon in front of her, and the interested gaze of a large woman stuffed into a red dress fixed on her with fish-eyed curiosity.

And if he left she'd never see him again. She didn't know how or why she knew that, but she did.

'No,' she said, with a bright, forced smile that he didn't seem to notice. 'Of course I don't. Any more than you love me.'

He gave her a look so cool and composed, it nearly broke her heart, and said in a low voice, 'That's all right, then.' A little while later, he swallowed a mouthful of champagne and added impassively, 'Well? Have you made up your mind? Is it to be a long engagement eventually broken? Or marriage with no strings attached?'

Angela smiled shakily. 'You sound

terribly cold-blooded about it. And I never did see the advantage to you.'

He smiled back, a strange, weary smile that tugged at her heartstrings. 'Neither did I altogether. Except that it will please my loving family. But you assured me you never got engaged unless you had marriage in mind. And I have to admit it will give me great pleasure to close off one of Caley Cove's hottest hotlines. They've had nearly twenty years' worth of solid-gold scuttlebut out of me.'

He reached across the table to take her hand, and when she looked into his winter-grey eyes common sense deserted her as usual. 'Yes,' she said. 'All right. Let's do it.'

'You make it sound like a suicide pact,' said Ryan drily. 'Believe me, my angel, I have no intention of joining you in a hemlock party.'

The strangeness had gone from his eyes now, and Angela laughed.

They finished lunch without further engaging the interest of the Red Lady, and afterwards, as Ryan had promised, they walked for miles — along the peaceful shores of the lake, and up the steep, forested path to Marymere Falls where Angela knew Sarah and Brett had once pursued their courtship.

By the time they climbed into the Alfa-Romeo to drive home, Angela was footsore, pleasantly sleepy, and hopeful that her daily exercise routine would keep her joints from stiffening up next day.

Later, Charlotte plied them with cups of tea and the pronouncement that no nephew of hers need think he was getting married by a Justice of the Peace. A nice church wedding it would be, she said firmly. At St Matthew's. With a choir. And nice flowers. And bridesmaids.

'My sister, and Sarah and Faith,' said Angela placatingly. She'd known they'd never get away with Ryan's idea of a small, family wedding. Her own mother would choke on the idea too, even though it was the second time around.

How long ago, and how unimportant, that other wedding seemed.

'And a best man.' Charlotte turned her attention to Ryan.

'He'll ask Rob,' muttered Harry resignedly. 'And *he'll* probably turn up in hiking boots — '

'Martin Cody,' said Ryan succinctly. 'And, Dad, I do have a couple of friends outside of the criminal fraternity. Not many. I'm not a social animal. But enough.' Although he was smiling, Angela realised it would take time for this father and son to recover completely from the years of suspicion and resentment. Perhaps Ryan's marriage would speed up the process. The thought pleased her.

It was dark when he pulled the car into her driveway after they'd enjoyed a substantial meal cooked by Aunt Charlotte. Angela felt a little tense. Was Ryan going to insist on coming in? And if he did, was she going to let him . . . ? She allowed the thought to trail off because she didn't know whether to welcome it or fight it. It wasn't easy being engaged to a man who didn't, or couldn't, love you back.

But when the car stopped, he only dropped a hand loosely on to her shoulder and bent down to peck her on the cheek. 'It's late,' he said lightly. 'Dad and Aunt Charlotte will think the worst if I don't rejoin them. I'll call you.'

'Yes.' Angela nodded, fumbled with the handle, and tumbled on to the gravel before he had a chance to get out. 'Thank you. It's been a — a nice day.'

Ryan smiled wryly. 'Spoken just like my favourite aunt. No wonder I asked you to marry me.' He lifted a hand in farewell, and Angela laughed softly and ran up the path to the door.

When she fitted the key in the lock, she noticed the car was still in the driveway. But once she stepped into the narrow hall all thought of Ryan was swept from her mind. There was a strange smell coming from the kitchen. She reached for the light switch and hurried across the hall.

Smoke was trailing around the edges of her oven, attaching itself to the walls and turning them grey. Angela groaned. The bean casserole she'd put in that morning, intending to freeze it as soon as it cooled — she'd forgotten all about it. Could she have turned on the timer out of habit? She groaned again. Stupid question. Obviously she had done precisely that.

Seizing a pot-holder in one hand and holding her nose with the other, she advanced through the smoke to grab the oven door. Al nattered crossly from the other room as she pulled out a pot of cremated beans.

Muttering under her breath and holding the pot at arm's length, Angela marched outside to the waste-bin. It wasn't until she was returning to the house that from the corner of her eye she caught a glimpse of something white in the driveway.

The Alfa-Romeo was still there. With its engine running.

10

Angela paused, and unconsciously pressed a hand to her heart. Ryan hadn't gone. What was he doing here? Something must be wrong.

Slowly, the burnt pot still clutched in her hands, she walked down the driveway to the car.

He was sitting with his arms round the steering-wheel and his head bowed on his hands.

'What's the matter?' she asked. 'Aren't you well?'

He looked up, an odd, haunted expression on his face, as though for a moment he wasn't sure who she was. Then his features cleared, and he said calmly, 'I was thinking.'

'What about?'

'Us. You and me. And about how something I never thought could happen has come to pass.' He spoke with very little emphasis, but Angela suspected the soft words concealed a baffled frustration. When he added more aggressively, 'And what the devil are *you* doing out here?' she knew she was right.

'I set the timer on the oven before I left the house this morning. By mistake. I've just been throwing out the charred remains of what was supposed to be a Creole bean casserole.'

Ryan frowned. 'You could have burned the place down.'

'Thanks for telling me. I'd never have thought of that myself.' It was late, she was tired, and she didn't need some patronising man telling her what she already knew. Particularly this patronising man.

'Don't be sarcastic,' he said wearily.

This time it was Angela's turn to frown, because now that she looked at him more closely she could see that in the pale light of the moon he looked haggard and desperately tired. She remembered he'd been working very hard.

'You'd better come in and have some coffee,' she said abruptly. 'You look much too worn out to drive.'

She thought perhaps he would argue — that, like so many men, he would take any doubt cast on his driving ability as an insult to his masculinity. But he didn't. He merely nodded and said, 'You're probably right.'

Ten minutes later his long body was draped across her sofa and she was setting a tray of coffee and biscuits down beside him. But when she started to hand him a mug, she saw that his eyes were already closed. Quietly she put the mug back on the tray and went to pick up the brown leather jacket he'd allowed to fall in a heap on the floor.

As she hung it carefully over the back of a wooden chair, his wallet fell out of the pocket. She picked it up, and saw something white lying on the carpet.

It was a photograph of a young woman with huge gypsy eyes and short brown hair. Without thinking, Angela turned the picture over to see if the young woman had a name.

She had. It was Connie. And above her signature she had written a few words:

To Ryan, who put another woman's happiness before mine, and didn't love me enough to clear his name. Goodbye, and thanks for the memories.

Angela gasped, dropped the picture and stumbled against the chair, knocking it over. As she bent to right it, she saw that Ryan's eyes were open and fixed on her with wide-awake suspicion.

'What are you doing?' he demanded.

'I was hanging up your jacket. Your wallet — and this — fell out.' She showed him the picture.

'I see.'

She knew at once that he thought she'd been prying, and weariness, melded with the unhappy misgivings she'd been suffering from all day, made her say sharply, 'No, you don't. You don't see at all. The picture fell on the floor and I picked it up. And yes, I read the back. But I didn't mean to, and I'm not about to apologise. Here.' She handed it to him. 'I certainly don't want it.'

Ryan gazed up at her, his eyes no longer suspicious, but flat and distant. 'Aren't you going to ask who she is?'

'No. You'll tell me if you want me to know.' She turned away, not wanting him to see that he had hurt her.

He didn't reply, and she was just about to go back into the kitchen when she felt his hands on her wrist and his warm breath teasing her hair.

'Angela. Come and sit down. You have a right to know why Connie wrote that message. It's just not something I choose to talk about in the normal course of events.' He turned her around and steered her back to the sofa.

Angela sat beside him, not touching, but with her hands in her lap as she stared into the empty fireplace. After a while Ryan said, 'Connie was the woman I hoped to marry. Many years ago. She left me when she found out I had it in my power to clear my name and refused to do it. I think she felt I owed it to her to offer her my unsullied reputation. Hence the photo and its message.'

Angela looked briefly at his face, which gave nothing away, and then turned back to the fireplace. 'But why wouldn't you do as she asked? For your own sake and your father's as well? I know you said you didn't want to waste any more of your life fighting the system, but — '

'But if that was my only problem, why couldn't I make the effort for the sake of the woman I loved? Unfortunately it wasn't that simple.'

'No,' said Angela. 'It wouldn't be.' Nothing was ever simple with Ryan.

He threw her a sharp glance, but she wasn't looking at him, so he went on as if she hadn't spoken. 'It was about a year after I got out of gaol, and I'd recently parted from a young lady called Amy, who ran for cover the moment I told her I'd done time. Connie knew about my sentence, and at first she didn't seem to mind. I began to dream . . . ' His mouth angled up in a bitter curve. 'I hadn't learned then that dreams vanish when you try to hold on to them. Because I was young, relatively inexperienced and of course burning up with unused hormones, it goes without saying that I fell heavily. Then I got a letter from a woman who said she'd had a religious conversion and wanted to clear her conscience. It turned out she'd witnessed the incident that put me away. And she was convinced I wasn't to blame. She hadn't come forward at the time because she was married, and she'd been at the pool hall with a boyfriend. The letter said her marriage had survived, happily, believe it or not, but that her husband would be devastated by a media circus focusing on her affair — the inevitable result of any overt campaign to clear my name. Even so, she was willing to make a public statement of my behalf.'

'And you wouldn't take her up on it?' Angela twisted round to frown her bewilderment at him, and saw that the muscles of his face were pulled tight.

'No.' He met her look with something like a challenge, as if he was daring her to argue. 'When I first received the letter I was angry. Her evidence could have kept me out of gaol. But when I went to see her, I met a sweet, guilt-ridden creature who had undoubtedly suffered for her silence, and was, belatedly, I grant you, willing to suffer a lot more to put things right. And suddenly I didn't see the point. I figured I'd caused enough grief. I was getting on with my studies and my life and there was no good reason to destroy some other man's happiness.' The edge of his mouth lifted. 'Besides, it was my one and only chance to play the martyr.'

'But — Connie. And your father . . . '

'At the time I had no contact with my

father. I foolishly believed he didn't care.' Ryan smiled, a wry, sad smile that caused a sudden pricking behind her eyelids. 'If it makes you feel any better, he and Aunt Charlotte have seen the letter. And they agree with me that there was no point in reopening an old wound, making others suffer merely to have my name cleared officially and publicly.' His lips curved with a cynical detachment. 'My father, of all people, knew that Caley Cove would never accept my innocence — I'd caused too much trouble in my youth — and he'd long since grown used to living with the sympathy showered on him by the good gossips of this town. I think he'd come to expect and even enjoy it. But in case you're wondering, yes, unofficially I did show the letter to one or two people who mattered. I've never regretted my decision to leave it at that.'

'But surely Connie — '

'Connie didn't understand. In a way I can't blame her. Looking back on it, I should have seen that she was attracted to me at first mainly *because* of my reputation. She was only twenty, and I suppose I was part of the teenage rebellion she hadn't really outgrown. Then reality set in, she met a medical student everyone said was destined to go far, and she realised she had to make up her mind between a lawyer about whom there would always be whispers and a man who was likely to attract nothing but admiration.'

'But if she loved you — '

'She didn't, of course. She only thought she did for a while. The letter brought that home to her, I think. In the end it provided a convenient excuse for choosing her medical student. Poor fellow.' Ryan linked his hands behind his head and gazed up at the ceiling with a curious emptiness in his eyes.

'Oh,' said Angela as understanding dawned. 'So that's why you don't believe in love, why you can give a woman your body but not your trust — '

'No!' He sat up suddenly and gripped

her arm. 'No, angel, don't ever think that. The point isn't that I don't trust people — though perhaps I don't much — but that I know I can trust myself. And I don't want anyone counting on me as any kind of rock in a storm. I've let enough people down for one lifetime, and I don't mean for it to happen again. I keep Connie's photo to remind myself that love is only a trap for the unwary. If I'd done as she wanted and used that letter to exonerate myself, we'd probably have ended up married. It would have been a disaster. She'd have gone on wanting me to be someone I couldn't be, and I'd have despised myself for destroying that unfortunate husband's happy marriage.'

Angela wrenched her arm away and shifted to the other end of the sofa. 'You mean you believe there is such a thing?' she asked, trying to keep the sarcasm out of her voice. Ryan didn't need sarcasm. He needed something to shake him out of his ruthless self-reliance. But she couldn't provide it.

Nobody could. His character had been forged in too much pain. His childhood, his lost young manhood, being falsely blamed for the death of another man, gaol, Connie — then gradual rehabilitation and years spent fighting to keep other young men from taking the path he had followed. He had seen and suffered too much to change now.

But Ryan was a strong, compassionate man, and always had been, or he wouldn't have balked at destroying a marriage whose happiness he couldn't even believe in.

'Sure,' he said now, brutally confirming her conclusions. 'I believe there's such a thing as a happy marriage. Provided neither party is dumb enough to think they're in love. That's why I'm willing to believe that you and I will manage very well.'

Angela didn't want to manage. She wanted the dream he didn't believe in. The dream she hadn't believed in herself for a long time. But she had changed. Love could do that to a person, it seemed. Only Ryan didn't love her, and he wouldn't change.

Sadly she reached for his mug of coffee, now almost cold, poured it back into the carafe and went into the kitchen to heat it in her microwave oven.

When she returned to the living-room, she half expected to find Ryan asleep. But to her surprise he was sitting with a ruffled-looking Al perched on the end of his finger. The two of them seemed to be engaged in a game of Who's going to be the first to blink? She paused to watch them.

Al won with ease, and Angela took him and perched him on her shoulder from where he hopped at once to her head.

Ryan raised his eyebrows and grinned, and after that it was impossible to carry on a serious conversation.

Besides, there was no more to be said.

★   ★   ★

Angela poked doubtfully at a poached egg and looked across the table at Ryan. He was staring with equal scepticism at the congealed remains of breakfast on his plate.

By the time the two of them had finished their coffee last night, it had been very late. Ryan had seemed disinclined to move, and Angela hadn't had the heart to make him leave. When the sun had begun to rise above the trees in a pale, glowing flood of pink, she had decided there wasn't much sense in going to bed, and offered him breakfast.

He had accepted after a moment's hesitation, eaten without speaking, and now seemed absorbed by a thin river of solidifying egg yolk.

Angela gazed at the top of his head. 'What's the matter?' she asked. 'Having second thoughts?'

He pushed at a piece of toast with his fork. 'About what?'

'This farce of an engagement, of course. You don't have to go on with it, you know.'

'So you keep saying. With a monotonous lack of originality. If you're attempting to bore me into changing my mind, it may yet work.'

He sounded so sarcastic and bitter that Angela wasn't sure whether she should throw the salt shaker at him on the principle of salting his wounds, or move round the table to gather him into her arms. In the end she did neither, and after a while Ryan lifted his head.

'That was uncalled for,' he said flatly. 'I'm sorry.'

'Why so glum?' she asked, more gently now because she could see how exhausted he was and she didn't want him to relapse into silence.

He shrugged, and even after a sleepless night Angela felt her stomach lurch at the movement of muscles swelling beneath his shirt. His eyes were far-away and grey as lead. 'I guess lack of sleep has just delivered a health-giving shot of reality.'

'In what way?' asked Angela.

'I'm beginning to see that you were right. A marriage of inconvenience won't work.'

Her heart thumped down to her knees. Of course she was right. But she had wished so much that she could be wrong. 'No,' she agreed dully. 'It probably won't. But surely that doesn't bother the man who doesn't believe in commitment.'

Ryan threw her a sardonic glance. 'No. It doesn't really. Which leaves us with one of two choices.'

Angela ran her tongue over her lips. 'Which are?'

He gave an impatient sigh, and banged his forehead with his fist. 'I take it back. There's only one choice, isn't there?'

Angela didn't need to ask what that choice was. Ryan wanted to call the whole thing off. Which, of course, was the sensible thing to do. But she found she didn't want to be sensible. She wanted to change the subject so that, just for the moment, she could sit finishing her morning coffee with Ryan, pretend mornings would be this way forever, and not think at all about the future.

Besides, all at once she was incredibly tired.

'Ryan,' she said slowly. 'Do you think . . . ?' She stopped, unable to recall what she'd meant to say.

Ryan's eyes narrowed. 'Angel, are you all right?'

'Yes, of course, I . . . '

Suddenly the room started to swim round in front of her eyes. When she looked down, the egg on her plate had turned into a canary. But she didn't have a canary. Al was a grey and bedraggled cockatiel. Who couldn't sing. As her head fell forward into her breakfast, she heard him say, 'Grack,' several times.

Ryan said, 'Hell and damnation,' and picked her up in his arms.

★ ★ ★

When Angela awoke, the sun was low in the sky and she knew it must be late afternoon. She was lying on top of her bed in her bra and panties, and Ryan, wearing only his briefs, was lying beside her. Or half lying. It was a single bed, and one of his legs was trailing on the floor. His arm was thrown across her chest, and he was fast asleep. He must have been even more exhausted than she was, because she was certain nothing had happened between them while she slept. She would have known in spite of her exhaustion.

Very gently, she moved his arm and sat up. He stirred, and muttered something in his sleep, but he didn't wake.

She gazed down at him, at the long eyelashes tracing the curve of a cheek that wasn't as hard-edged in repose. At the tawny-gold hair falling tousled across his neck and forehead, and at the soft, sensual line of his lips. He looked so peaceful, so vulnerable, lying here beside her — not at all the contained and guarded man she knew.

As she watched the slow rise and fall

of his chest then saw him move his hand as if he was searching for something, she was overcome with a terrible, aching tenderness for this difficult man. She touched a finger to his lips, followed the full curve with despair in her heart, because she knew that the time had come to bid farewell to the foolish hope that had allowed her to accept his proposal. He had asked her to marry him for his father's sake, not for his own — and also because he was concerned for her reputation in this town where she earned her living but which he hated. Ryan was strong and incorruptible, but his past had destroyed something in him, had deprived him of the ability to surrender his heart to another except, perhaps, for a few stolen moments of passion.

He had already admitted that their marriage couldn't work, that the idea had been a mistake. He didn't want her love. So surely the only thing she could do for him now was make sure he never knew how much she cared — let him leave her quietly without embarrassing goodbyes. But if he woke up now she was almost certain to betray what she felt for him. She wouldn't be able to dissimulate any longer, because the pain was too recent and too real.

Her eyes very wide, willing the tears to stay back, Angela eased herself carefully off the bed. Her crumpled mauve print dress lay over a chair, and she pulled it on before stumbling out to the kitchen.

A pad of paper lay conveniently on the counter and she picked up a pencil and began to write.

Dear Ryan, Thank you for the happy times. I know you meant everything for the best, but of course you were right when you said earlier that a marriage of inconvenience couldn't work. To save post-mortems, I've decided to spend a few days with my parents. Could you ask Rob to cancel my appointments? Help yourself to food. I've taken Al with me. Good luck with the boot case and — take care. Angela.

The 'take care' was an unreadable scrawl, because the pencil had wanted to write, I love you, and she hadn't let it.

After that she found a pair of sandals in the hall cupboard, picked up her bag and Al's cage, and, last of all, tiptoed to the door of the bedroom.

Ryan was lying on his stomach now with one arm stretched across the bed as if she were still there beside him.

A great lump swelled in her chest, and she closed her eyes and turned away. If she stayed a moment longer, she'd never leave.

Barely seeing where she was going, she staggered outside and eased herself into the Buick. Al, in his cage beside her, made soft, protesting noises in his throat.

For a moment Angela let her head drop on to the steering-wheel. When she lifted it, dark clouds were gathering over the mountains.

The heatwave was over.

* * *

'Damn,' muttered Angela.

This was all she needed. Ahead of her on the road leading from Caley Cove on to the highway a huge semi-trailer was skewed sideways, blocking access. Behind it, a line of vehicles was steadily growing.

A middle-aged man with a beard, not bothering to temper his language, heaved himself out of the car in front of her and started shouting obscenities at the driver of the trailer, who was leaning out of his cab.

'Shuddup,' the driver bellowed back. 'You think you can fix it, go ahead.'

'Got your licence out of a popcorn box, did you?' yelled the car owner.

A woman who had just pulled up behind Angela added her voice to the dispute, and soon half the occupants were out of their vehicles and shouting. The driver of the trailer, rising to the provocation, jumped on to the road and started shaking his fists.

'Oh, why don't you all shut up and let him get on with getting it back on the road?' moaned Angela, clinging hard to the wheel of the Buick. She couldn't bear all this noise. All she wanted was to get on with her journey and return to the loving arms of her family. With them she might regain some kind of peace.

'Grack, grack, grack,' said Al, adding to the general cacophany.

Angela groaned and covered her eyes, and in a moment she heard rain pinging on to the metal roof of her car. Reaching for the handle of the driver's window, she started to roll it up. It wouldn't budge. Sighing, she turned to examine it — and found herself looking straight into a pair of smoky eyes. They were a hard, chilling pewter, and she knew at once that their owner was no happier than she was. In fact he reminded her of a tawny-haired pirate looking for a handy throat to cut.

His hand was pushing down on the top of her window. 'Get out,' snapped Ryan.

Angela stared at his face. It was more parchment than gold in this light, and the warm lips she had caressed so lovingly were bloodless. She wasn't convinced it would be safe to get out.

11

'Ryan,' whispered Angela.

'Get out,' he repeated.

When she didn't respond, he yanked the door open, bent down, and dragged her into his arms.

She opened her mouth to protest, and he closed it with a blistering kiss.

After that the world ceased to exist for Angela outside the magic square of ground where she stood locked in her lover's arms, oblivious to the rain, the angry drivers, and the growing line of traffic. All she knew was that he was kissing her as he had never kissed her before, and that she wanted him to go on doing it forever. She didn't even remember that she had been trying to escape him.

But when he held her roughly away and said, 'What the devil do you mean by running out on me?' she came down to earth so fast she would have fallen if he hadn't been gripping her elbows.

She gulped, and fixed her gaze on the wet shirt plastered to his chest. 'It was in the note,' she mumbled. 'No post-mortems.'

'I'll give you post-mortems,' he growled, raking a hand through her rain-soaked brown hair. 'The post-mortem to end all post-mortems.' He glanced down at the dress that clung saturated and revealing to every shivering curve of her slender body, and added forcefully, 'Or I will if I get the chance before this mob gets the idea that you're a free gift provided by the god of traffic jams for the entertainment and consolation of his male victims.'

Angela looked round and saw that several of the men had indeed been distracted from the fray, and were leaning out of their cars eyeballing her wetly outlined figure.

'That's your fault,' she said. 'You pulled me out into the rain and got me soaked, and now I'm stuck here — '

'No, you're not. Start walking back down the road. My car's round the corner facing home. I'll pull yours off to the side. We can collect it tomorrow.'

When she didn't move, but stood staring up at him with her mouth open, he turned her round and gave her a smart shove to get her started. 'Go on. I'll catch you up.'

'But I'm going to Tacoma,' she protested over her shoulder.

'You are not going to Tacoma. You'd have pneumonia by the time you got there. Apart from which, you and I have some business to settle.'

She turned to look at him, and saw that he was already sliding into her car. The angle of his jaw was not accommodating.

The heavens opened further, moulding her hair to her head like wet satin. The semi-trailer was still blocking the road, although the driver was at least making some effort to shift it. 'Oh, very well,' she said, to the surprise of an adolescent ogling her from the window of his van. 'I suppose there's nothing else for it.'

Wet, still reeling from Ryan's kisses, and not sure whether she wanted to laugh or burst into tears, she staggered along the verge to the corner.

Just as she rounded it, Ryan came up behind her. His chest was bare, and his damp white shirt was draped protectively over Al's cage. He put a dripping wet arm around her waist. A moment later he was pressing her unceremoniously into the Alfa-Romeo, and then he was swinging himself down beside her and speeding along the rain-slicked road that led to home.

As soon as they were back inside the house, Ryan placed a disgruntled Al on his table and pushed Angela, who was standing in the hallway looking stupefied, into her bedroom.

'Out of that dress and into something dry,' he ordered.

Angela, slowly emerging from her fog, turned round and said dully, 'I'm not a child, Ryan. And what about you?

You're soaked to the skin.'

'Don't worry about me. I'll manage. And by the way, I *had* noticed you're all grown-up.'

She glanced at his face, wondering if she'd really heard that teasing note in his voice, but his features were as unreadable as ever. Sighing, she went into the bedroom to change.

When she emerged, wrapped in a white cotton robe, Ryan was standing in front of the stove making tea.

Angela, gazing dazedly at the brief blue towel that barely came to the top of his thighs, had to remind herself that she wasn't supposed to be wishing he'd forget about tea and start making her instead.

She also had to remind herself that she wanted him out of her house, because if he stayed around much longer she was sure to give away just how much she loved him — needed him even.

'I'm all right now,' she told him. 'You don't have to stay any longer. I know you have to get back to Seattle.'

'Yes, I do.' He went on preparing the tea, and when it was ready he lifted the pot and set it on the table. 'Sit down.' He waved at a chair.

Angela gave up and sat down. Having made her momentous decision to let Ryan go, and failed miserably, she now seemed incapable of making up her mind about anything. Vaguely, she was aware that sooner or later she would have to take charge of her life again. But not just this minute. Not with Ryan looking devastating and determined across the table.

'OK,' he said. 'What was that all about?'

'I wanted to make it easy for you,' she said truthfully. 'You'd admitted a marriage between us couldn't work. So I thought it would be best if we parted without fuss or embarrassing goodbyes.'

Ryan rested his forearms on the table and linked his fingers loosely together. 'I didn't say a marriage between us couldn't work.'

'But — '

'I said a marriage of inconvenience couldn't work. It's not the same thing.'

'No,' agreed Angela doubtfully. 'I suppose not, but — '

'But it won't be inconvenient, will it? Not if you love me?' His eyes were like charcoal, deep, immovable and intense.

'I . . . ' She swallowed, tried to look away and found she couldn't. 'I — don't . . . ' She wasn't able to finish.

'Don't you? That's not what you said in your sleep.' His voice was as deadpan as his face, but when she looked down at his hands she saw that he was clenching them so tightly together that the skin across his knuckles had turned paper-white. 'Oh,' she whispered. 'Did I? But — that was only a dream. I may have said it in the heat of the moment, but . . . '

Ryan was shaking his head. 'No,' he said. 'You spoke very clearly and slowly. Because you meant it. I think perhaps you knew I was there. Now look me straight in the eye and tell me that isn't the truth.'

Angela looked him in the eye. His gaze was fixed and immovable, but just for a moment she thought she saw a shade of total defencelessness, as if his very life hinged on her answer. The look vanished quickly, but she had seen it.

Why, he *wants* me to love him, she thought, unable to grasp the meaning of what she'd seen. But why . . . ? She dropped her head into her hands. Was it possible . . . ? No. It couldn't be. And yet . . .

She looked up. Ryan hadn't moved. He was waiting, silent and still as a rock, for her to speak. And she had no choice but to tell him what he wanted to hear. What she had longed to tell him for weeks.

'Yes,' she said. 'It is the truth, of course. I do love you.'

Instead of responding, Ryan closed his eyes.

When he didn't open them at once, Angela said frantically, 'But it's all right. You needn't worry — that's why I was running away.'

At that he did open his eyes, very slowly, and his mouth stretched into the laziest, sexiest, most heartwarming smile she had ever seen. 'I'm not worrying any more,' he said, in that low, slow drawl she loved so much. He held out his hands. 'Come here.'

Mesmerised, Angela stood up and moved round the table towards him. The room seemed very quiet all of a sudden, and it was a few seconds before she took in that the rain had stopped.

When she reached his side, he put both hands on her waist and drew her on to his knee. Then he kissed her for a very long time.

This time it was Angela who pulled away first. 'Ryan,' she murmured, her voice muffled against his shoulder, 'I don't understand. I thought — '

'So did I,' he said, lifting her chin and forcing her to look right at him. 'And I was a damn fool.'

'What do you mean?' She was trying to conquer a ridiculous urge to cry.

'I mean that I love you quite

desperately, my angel, and it's taken me far too long to realise that's the only thing that matters in this life.' His eyes softened and his thumb traced the outline of her mouth. 'Love and friendship, and being there for the one you love when she needs you, are far more important than any safe and passionless independence. I suppose, in a way, I've known that from the moment I met you. It has to be why I proposed that crazy mockery of a marriage — as a way of having my cake and eating it as well.' His voice changed, became husky. 'But when I woke up and found you gone, it came to me like a blow in the stomach — or a well-placed kick in the right place — that I couldn't bear to live my life without you.'

Suddenly he wrapped his arm around her and pressed her cheek against his. 'That was when I knew, however unwillingly, that I had come to need you, and to depend on you, my beloved and outspoken angel. On your love, so generously expressed in your sleep, and on your trust and loyalty for always. In the end I think it took me only a very few seconds to throw off the thinking of half a lifetime. But you'd already gone.'

He gave her an improbably guileless look then cleared his throat. 'Luckily I ran into an old client of mine a few days ago. He's driving a semi-trailer now.'

'You didn't!' Angela gasped and sat upright.

'Mm. Caught him just as he was about to leave town.'

'Oh! You mean there was nothing wrong with his engine?'

'Not to my knowledge.' Ryan leaned back, smiling with impenitent complacence.

'You conniving, underhanded, devious — '

'Crook?' he suggested helpfully. 'I know. My naturally felonious instincts come in handy once in a while.'

Angela frowned. He had reminded her of something that still hung unexpressed and unexplained between them. Ryan saw the frown and immediately tipped her off his knee.

'Yes,' he said, suddenly grim-faced. 'You want to know, don't you?'

Angela smoothed her hands nervously down her hips. 'Know?' she repeated.

'If it's safe to trust me around knives.'

He sounded so cold, the old, frozen Ryan she knew too well, that all at once Angela discovered she couldn't face him. She turned on her heel and hurried out of the room. He caught up with her just as she was removing Al from his cage.

'Hold it,' he said. 'I want to talk to you. Put that damn bird down.'

'Al's not a 'damn bird'. And I thought you didn't approve of cages.'

'I don't. But in his case I have to admit the necessity. Put him on top of it.'

She put him on her shoulder.

Ryan shrugged. 'OK. What's he supposed to be? Bodyguard or moral support?'

'Both, I think,' said Angela.

He smiled crookedly. 'I'm not sure I like the sound of that. Come and sit down.' When she hesitated he said impatiently, 'Both of you,' and drew her over to the sofa.

'What is this?' she asked. 'Are you about to tell me — ?' She stopped. She had been going to say, Are you about to tell me you're the Caley Cove Ripper? but it didn't sound that funny after all.

'I'm about to tell you what happened that night,' he said, lowering himself down beside her and fixing his gaze on the raindrops drying on the window. Angela touched a hand to his cheek, and after a while he went on in a hard, strained tone she'd never heard him use before, 'It's something I try not to think about. There's no point. The whole mess was over and done with long ago, and there's nothing I can do to change the past.'

'But you told Connie . . . '

'Of course I told Connie. I wanted to marry her. She had every right to know what she was getting into. Just as you do.'

'Yes,' agreed Angela, hearing the note of tension and knowing he was finding it hard to speak. 'It must have been — difficult for you.'

'Yeah. You might say that.' He didn't look at her.

Suddenly Angela was frightened. She'd never heard Ryan say 'yeah' instead of 'yes' before. It made him sound like a stranger. What was he going to tell her? That he had, after all, murdered a man in cold blood? If it was that, would she feel the same about him? She had thought it wouldn't matter, but now, faced with revelation, she was afraid.

'You don't have to tell me,' she said quickly.

'Yes. I do. There will be no more secrets between us.' His tone was heavy, and Angela felt goose-bumps pricking at her skin. He was still glaring fixedly at the window.

She put up her hand to stroke Al.

'There was this guy called Jake,' Ryan said with sudden harshness. 'I'd won money off him at poker a couple of times, and he didn't like me for it, even though I'd won it fair and square. He seemed to blame me for his own bad play. He was a lot older than I was, of course. Made his living conning kind and gullible souls into giving him their money for some charity. Jake was the charity. Ironic, when you come to think of it.'

Angela was trying not to think of it, so she didn't answer.

'In any case,' Ryan went on, 'I'd heard that he was making threats against me, but, being young and immortal, I didn't take any notice. Then one night when I stepped out the back of the pool hall to get some air — my friends inside were finishing up a game — he jumped me. He was drunk and he had a knife in his hand. I grabbed his wrist and we fought, and somehow the knife got twisted round and ended up in his chest. I was trying to take it from him. In fact, I think he stabbed himself. That's what the woman who wrote the letter said. She'd been outside smooching with her boyfriend, and she saw it all after he left.' Ryan tore his gaze from the window and ran the back of his arm across his forehead. It was beaded with sweat. 'I wouldn't have killed him,' he said grimly. 'I didn't like Jake, but I wasn't a killer.'

'Oh, Ryan.' Angela put a hand on the nearest bunched shoulder, but he shrugged it off. 'Ryan, you're not still blaming yourself, are you? It wasn't your fault.'

'It was my fault I lived the sort of life I did. And had the kind of friends who carried knives.' He gave a laugh that Angela found far more chilling than the ugly story he had told her. 'Where else would you suggest I lay the blame?'

'I wouldn't. But — Jake was dead because he attacked you.' She clasped her hands between her knees, wanting desperately to touch him, but knowing he didn't want that. 'Ryan, I don't understand. It was obviously self-defence. How could you possibly have been convicted?'

'It wasn't obviously anything,' he said harshly. 'I was a known trouble-maker and I had no witness. Neither did the prosecution. Which was probably why the charge was reduced to manslaughter. Lucky for me.'

His voice was so choked with bitterness that Angela had to swallow hard to stop herself from bursting into tears. She didn't need to be told that the last thing he wanted was sweet sympathy.

'But you shouldn't have been convicted at all,' she protested. 'You couldn't have acted any other way.'

'I could have stayed out of trouble all along,' he replied bleakly. 'There was a damn good reason no one came forward to vouch for my exemplary character.'

'Yes, I see,' said Angela, who perhaps saw more than he intended.

She stared at his head, now turned away from her, and at the tawny-gold hair curling so rebelliously at his neck — and for the first time she really understood what had made Ryan into the tough, self-reliant man he was. A man who took responsibility for the mistakes of his past, and who had, by his own efforts, pulled himself out of the pit into which he'd descended to become an asset to the community where he lived. A human being who, without sentimentality, attempted to kick other losers like himself back on to the road that would lead them to make something of their lives.

A lesser man would have given up without a fight.

No wonder she had fallen in love with him. And no wonder he'd found it hard to respond.

He was staring at the carpet now, his forearms resting loosely on his knees. And it was time to forget the past and start on a very promising future.

'Don't look back, Ryan,' Angela said

softly. 'It's over.' She put her hand on his neck and began to massage it gently. This time he didn't shrug it off.

'It doesn't matter to you, does it?' he said quietly.

'What doesn't?'

'The fact that I've never had my name officially cleared. And probably never will. As far as I know, my witness is still with her husband.'

'No,' said Angela with a far-away smile. 'No, it doesn't matter. I'm not Connie, and I think you were right not to make that woman's husband suffer any more than he already had for her behaviour.'

'Thank you.' Ryan's eyes were very bright as he took her free hand and raised it to his lips.

Al, seeing a bridge to a fresh crop of hair that needed pulling, ran down his arm and hopped up on to his head.

'What the . . . ?' Ryan, sat up with a jerk, his face no longer flat and closed, but open-mouthed with surprise.

'It's only Al,' said Angela. 'Not a

giant vulture scenting a snack.'

Ryan's mouth snapped shut and he removed the little bird and held him balanced on his finger in front of his face. 'You,' he said to Al, 'are an ornithological menace. But I suppose you go with the deal.'

'What deal?' asked Angela.

'You. Is there any chance you come without the bird?'

'No,' said Angela, smiling. 'Al and I are partners.'

'Like hell. You're going to be partners with me.'

'Of course. We'll be a threesome.'

When Ryan started to tell her there was no way he was going into business with a bird, she laid her palm on his exposed thigh and began to stroke it. Al hopped down and began to pull at the towel.

'Damn bird,' muttered Ryan, covering her small hand with his large one.

'I told you, he's not a 'damn bird'.' Angela glanced at Al's struggles with the towel and smiled artlessly. 'Besides, you have to admit he does have some excellent ideas.' She removed the offending bird to return him to the top of his cage, and he gave a little 'grack' of disgust.

When she turned round, she found Ryan stretched out on the sofa wearing that sexy, heart-stopping smile again. He looked like a golden invitation to nirvana.

As Angela stood gazing down at him, her body limp with desire, he slid his hands slowly up under her white robe and, even more slowly, over her hips and thighs. She gasped, and, suddenly overwhelmed by her need for this beautiful man, stuttered idiotically, 'It — we haven't eaten. Shouldn't I make us some supper?'

'You should not,' he said, giving her a reproving look and pulling her summarily over on top of him. 'It's not food I want, my angel. It's you.' He began to push back the white robe. Angela squirmed voluptuously as he peeled it off and tossed it on to the floor. Then he put his hand on the back of her head and drew her mouth down to his.

With an ecstatic sigh, she reached for the blue towel and finished the job Al had started.

★ ★ ★

It was late September. The leaves were changing, and Angela could feel her body changing too.

She and Ryan had been married for only two months, and already she knew that another little Koniski was on the way. The tests had been confirmed that afternoon, but she hadn't yet had a chance to tell her husband.

The two of them were spending this weekend with Harry and Charlotte, but they had arranged to travel separately because Ryan was working late on a case. Angela had arrived early to oversee the transfer of her house and practice to a middle-aged family lawyer who had agreed to take Rob on as well.

As she gazed out of the window at

the bright heads of the daisies by the gate, she thought how fortunate she had been to unload her assets so quickly. She and Ryan had already bought a house on a hill in Seattle, and eventually she would be joining a city law firm which, at the back of her mind, she had half wanted to do for some time. But for now all she wanted was Ryan, and his child who was growing inside her.

Her eyes lit up when she saw her husband's car pull into the driveway, and with arms outstretched she hurried across the grass to greet him.

'You look like a Christmas tree,' he said, smiling down at her. 'Dressed in woodland green with all your lights turned on.'

'You turned them on,' she said softly.

Ryan thought how beautiful she was, and felt a strange pressure behind his eyes. Indeed to him she seemed to grow more beautiful each day. He wondered how he could ever have been fool enough to imagine he'd be able to let her go. Remembering his old, walled-in life, and contrasting it with the joy he took now in the days — and nights — filled with laughter and Angela's love, sometimes he still found it hard to believe it could last.

What a blind, pigheaded idiot he had been to imagine that life before his angel had been complete.

'We've been forgiven,' said the object of his musings, laughing up at him.

'Forgiven?' He raised his eyebrows, pretending he didn't know what she meant.

'Yes. For getting married without any fuss.'

'Ah. She's got over it, has she? I figured she would. Poor Aunt Charlotte.' He knew he ought to feel more repentent, but how could he possibly regret marrying Angela the first moment he could?

Charlotte had been furious, Harry relieved, and Angela's parents resigned, when Ryan had got his way and married his bride at St Matthew's in late July with only family and Martin and Sarah in attendance. He had explained that after waiting thirty-eight years to find the love of his life he was damned if he was waiting for a lot of discussion and commotion about guest lists, flowers, clothes, who would sit where and sing what, and whether they should serve canapés or real food. Angela had said that as far as she was concerned it wouldn't matter to her if they were married on Mars attended by giant robotic crabs.

'I've got news for you,' she told him now, fidgeting with his tie, and smiling a mysterious little smile.

'Sarah's had her baby,' Ryan guessed.

'Yes, a brother for Tony and Caroline. And I've just heard Faith's expecting too. But that's not — '

'The reproductive bug seems to be almost as efficient as the grapevine in this town,' he interrupted her with a grin. Lately he had found himself coming to terms with Caley Cove and its news network. After all, it had given him Angela.

As she smiled dreamily and wound her arms around his neck, Angela was thinking almost the same thing. Ryan looked at least ten years younger than the hard, world-weary man she had seen for the first time on that hot afternoon in early May.

After he had kissed her soundly, she held on to his shoulders and stood on tiptoe to whisper into his ear.

For a moment he appeared stunned, and then a huge grin slashed his handsome features as he took her face in his hands and began to kiss her all over again. By the time he'd finished Harry was standing on the steps watching them, so Ryan shouted at the top of his lungs, 'Dad, come on down here. Angela and I have something we want to tell you.'

Harry frowned and stomped across the grass towards them, his bushy hair more bristly than ever, and his pale eyes crinkling against the sun.

'What's all the noise about?' he demanded. 'More car trouble?'

'No,' said Ryan, grinning. 'No trouble at all for a change. Angela's going to have a baby.'

For a moment Harry's lined face seemed to crumple. Then he said in a voice so choked with emotion that they could scarcely hear it, 'A baby. You think a baby's no trouble?' He lowered his head, and Angela hoped the news wasn't going to be too much for him. But when he looked up there was a faint gleam of humour in his eye. 'Somehow I know everything will go right this time,' he said quietly. 'And I do believe I'm going to get my own back. Never thought I'd live to see the day.' Suddenly he put a hand on Ryan's arm, and there was an urgency in his tone and a dampness on his cheek that made Angela wonder what was coming next.

'If it's a girl,' he said, 'will you call her Laura?'

Ryan's mother's name. 'Yes, of course we will,' she said, not giving her husband time to answer. She smiled at the elderly man with the tears now pouring unashamedly down his face. 'It is a girl. I had tests done.'

Harry's mouth widened into a damp and beaming grin. It was as if the sun had come out after years of rain. 'Thank you,' he said, taking her hand and joining it with Ryan's. 'Thank you, my dear. Does Charlotte know?'

'Not yet. You were the first.'

His step as sprightly as a young man's, Harry hurried back into the house to spread the news.

'You've made us both very happy, my angel.'

Ryan was smiling at her with so much love and tenderness in his eyes that Angela felt a lump forming in her throat. 'I'm the luckiest woman in the world,' she whispered.

Ryan twined his fingers through her hair. 'And you've married the world's luckiest man.'

Mrs Gruber and Mavis Bracken, passing by on the other side of the street, were not impressed when Ryan gave them a casual wave before pulling Angela back into his arms to deliver another long and public kiss.

'Disgraceful,' muttered Mrs Gruber.

'Outrageous,' agreed Mavis Bracken wistfully.

'Quite scandalous,' said Ryan, looking up. 'Shall I do it some more?'

'Yes, please,' said Angela, linking her hands behind his neck.

Ryan did, very thoroughly. And when Mrs Gruber and Mavis Bracken turned round to get a better look, they were astounded to see him pick her up in his arms and carry her in laughing triumph up the path.

THE END

We do hope that you have enjoyed reading this large print book.

Did you know that all of our titles are available for purchase?

We publish a wide range of high quality large print books including:
Romances, Mysteries, Classics
General Fiction
Non Fiction and Westerns

Special interest titles available in large print are:
The Little Oxford Dictionary
Music Book, Song Book
Hymn Book, Service Book

Also available from us courtesy of Oxford University Press:
Young Readers' Dictionary
(large print edition)
Young Readers' Thesaurus
(large print edition)

For further information or a free brochure, please contact us at:
Ulverscroft Large Print Books Ltd.,
The Green, Bradgate Road, Anstey,
Leicester, LE7 7FU, England.
Tel: (00 44) **0116 236 4325**
Fax: (00 44) **0116 234 0205**

Other titles in the
Linford Romance Library:

MOMENT OF DECISION

Mavis Thomas

Benita is a dedicated doctor, but when questions about her professional competence arise following a street accident, she starts afresh as general assistant at Beacon House, a Children's Clinic. However, this brings new problems when she is faced with her boyfriend's disapproval, the Clinic's domineering but charismatic Superintendent, and the two disruptive children she befriends . . . and then she becomes the victim of a blackmailer! There are many urgent decisions to make before Benita's future becomes clear.

TO TRUST A STRANGER

Anne Hewland

When Sara Dent's landlord relinquishes his business interests to his great-nephew Matt Harding, Sara fears that she will lose control of her struggling craft shop. And what — or who — is causing the strange noises in the empty rooms above? As she becomes reluctantly attracted to Matt, she discovers that her sleepy market town conceals sinister secrets. Sara must undergo emotional upheaval and life-threatening danger before her true enemies are revealed, and she learns who can be trusted — and loved.

SHADOWED LOVE

Janet Thomas

Following a break-up with her partner, Helen Matthews returns to Cornwall to set up a bed and breakfast business in her inherited cottage. There, she meets the arrogant Martin Somerville, who offers to buy her land. Helen refuses, but she faces many more setbacks before she can realise her dream . . . And is it possible that she was wrong about Martin? Could they ever look forward to a future together?